THE ARCAV COMMANDER'S HUMAN

HOPE HART

Copyright © 2020 by Bingeable Books LLC

All rights reserved.

No part of this book may be reproduced in any form or by any electronic or mechanical means, including information storage and retrieval systems, without written permission from the author, except for the use of brief quotations in a book review.

The Arcav Alien Invasion Series

The Arcav King's Mate

The Arcav Commander's Human

The Arcav General's Woman

The Arcav Prince's Captive

A Very Arcav Christmas

The Arcav Captain's Queen

The Arcav Guard's Female

The Warriors of Agron Series

Taken by the Alien Warrior

Claimed by the Alien Warrior

Saved by the Alien Warrior

Seduced by the Alien Warrior

Protected by the Alien Warrior

Captured by the Alien Warrior

Rescued by the Alien Warrior

Enticed by the Alien Warrior

Conquered by the Alien Warrior

The Society of Savages Series

Wicked

Depraved

Brutal

❀ Created with Vellum

CHAPTER ONE

Amanda

I wake to pandemonium.

Am I...in hell?

Either that or it's the worst nightmare I've ever had.

I'm on a cold steel floor, and a buzzing sound is piercing my brain like a knife. My tongue feels like I've left my retainer in for three days and slept with my mouth open.

Women are crouched and lying in groups around me, some sobbing quietly, some rocking mindlessly, and some silent as the grave.

My head aches like it's been cracked open, and I reach up, checking for damage.

Nothing.

"What the fuck?" I mutter, slowly pushing myself up onto my knees. My sneakers are gone, but I'm still in my yoga pants and tank top. The last thing I remember is waiting for the lights to change on my way home from a late-night run.

Some of the other women weren't as lucky. A few of

them are in their underwear, and a couple are even naked, although a T-shirt goes flying across the room toward a woman currently looking down at her nude body in shock.

We're all relatively young women.

That alone tells me whatever is happening here probably isn't good. I push up further, pausing as I breathe through my mouth, fighting down bile. We're in a…cage.

No. No. No.

I stand up, and that's when I notice no one else is on their feet.

"Girl, get down. They'll hurt you!" The hushed voice comes from somewhere in a corner, and I ignore it.

"Where are we?" I ask the woman closest to me.

She scoots away. "I-I think it's some sort of alien ship. We've all been kidnapped. You were one of the last to wake up."

Halfway through her sentence, I slap my hands over my ears in a useless attempt to block her out. This can't be happening. Not to me.

Silence falls as a dark shape appears, opening the door to the cage.

"Sit." The voice is a cross between a growl and a mumble, although I can understand—thanks to the translators the Arcav ensured were inserted into our ears when they invaded Earth.

I stay standing—not because I'm brave but because I'm frozen in shock as the creature steps into the light.

I've seen Grivath on TV as politicians debate over which alien race poses the biggest threat to humanity—these guys or the Arcav.

Looking at this huge, hulking gray male with the massive teeth, my vote is for the former.

"Where are we?" I ask, and gasps ring throughout the cell.

He steps forward, and his grin is terrible. "Nowhere near your planet."

I can't breathe.

Before I know what's happening, I'm running at him like a wild animal, screaming.

"Let me go home! I need to go home!" I launch myself through the air, fist clenched as I swing at him. He simply grins wider and unholsters his weapon, and I go down, hitting the floor like a fallen tree.

I don't know how much time passes before I can do more than lie frozen in place as tears trickle down my cheeks. My limbs are dead weight. Will this paralysis last for the rest of—what is sure to be—my short and excruciating life?

"You okay, girl? You sure hit hard." I feel a hand brush my shoulder, and I reach for my words.

"My sister." I'm slurring like I've been on a three-day bender.

She rubs my shoulder harder, her hand warm. "Is she here?"

"No," I say, and the words are like a cliff I want to jump off. "She's dying."

Jaret

I know what it looks like.

When the Arcav commander insists on taking a mission that would otherwise be left to a general, hushed whispers and confused looks are to be expected.

Do I know why I demanded to handle the Grivath kidnapping of humans myself? No. All I know is my interest was sparked for the first time in decades.

When you live in a cold black-and-white world where each day is just like the last, you jump at the chance to feel something, anything other than rage.

"Commander."

I look up from my desk, where I'm analyzing the movements of the Grivath. The fact they have managed to acquire the best available cloaking system in this galaxy has changed our strategy considerably. "Yes?"

Roax stands at attention. "We're approaching the Grivath ship."

"Have you heard from the men we left in Gule?"

He hesitates for a moment, and then his shoulders droop. "Yes, Commander. One of the human women was killed attempting to escape. Another was severely injured. Yet another has gone missing, likely attempting her own escape. Both the Gulians and our men are looking for her now."

"How many humans were sold in Gule?"

"Around twenty or thirty."

Knowing the Grivath, I would lay wager they have kept at least a few humans to sell in Durin.

I lean back in my seat.

In this universe, there are two types of creatures: the hunter and the prey. If you are unlucky enough to be prey, it is best to be so anywhere but in Durin.

Durin is this galaxy's toilet, where hope goes to die. It's where evil souls purchase living beings for pleasure...and for pain.

The Grivath will unload some of their humans in Gule, which is a dirty, dangerous pit. But at least it's a dirty, dangerous pit with rules. Because after Gule, they'll move to Durin, where the only rule is "he with the most weapons wins." There, they can get ten times the price for the humans, if they're bold enough to risk both the journey and the locals on arrival.

And they will be.

When it comes to the Grivath, it's personal. My quest for revenge has been the only thing that gets me up in the morning. I won't be content until their planet is a wasteland.

"Prepare for boarding."

Amanda

The girl who spoke kindly to me is called Charlotte, although she told me to call her Charlie. She's tiny, built like a fairy—all big eyes and curly hair. But appearances are obviously deceptive, and while many of the women around us fall apart, she's whispering details about our captors in my ear, hoping we can come up with a way to escape.

Right now I'm useless, incapable of doing anything other than drooling on the floor and choking out the occasional word.

My father used to say my many sins would catch up with me one day.

Maybe he was right.

Don't fall apart. Don't fall apart.

I lie there for what feels like hours, fighting the claustrophobia that overwhelms me as I try and fail to move my limbs. Eventually, I close my eyes and play the listing game.

The listing game is something I've done ever since I can remember. I'd whisper to myself after dinner when we were kids while my father made us kneel on the hardwood floor for an hour of prayer.

Fall in DC. Fresh cookies. Bree attempting to remember the punchline of a joke.

Someone begins to sob loudly.

Trips to New York. The ocean. Watching Moulin Rouge.

Shrieks sound, and I tense, attempting to lift my head off the floor.

Charlie helps me roll onto my side, and we huddle together as a group of Grivath enter the cage. It seems like they're picking women at random, pulling them up, and carrying them out of the cage. They ignore their screams and shrieks, and I freeze as the asshole who stunned me stalks up to us.

He grabs hold of Charlie, who fights like a wild thing, but she doesn't have a chance against the beast. She manages to punch him in the nose as he lifts her, and he roars, slaps her across the face, and throws her over his shoulder. I push up on my hands, desperate to help, but he simply shoves me back down with a foot that smells like old cat food.

"You stay, human scum. You go to Durin."

From the sick pleasure on his face, I'm guessing Durin isn't a place I want to go. I watch helplessly as he hands Charlie to another Grivath, collects a few more women, and slams the cage door shut behind him.

Playing volleyball in the sun. Drinking margaritas in Cancun. That time Bree got stuck in a dress at H&M and we laughed until we almost peed our pants.

There's around twenty of us left, and silence falls after the Grivath are gone. Who knows what those assholes are going to do with the human women they took? But it's not looking good for any of us.

Later, we're given water but no food. I sit, rocking, bargaining with a God I no longer believe in.

I'll stop hating my father. I'll go to church. I'll be a born-again virgin. Anything. Just let me get back to Bree.

Hushed voices discuss how we ended up on this ship and where we're going.

"How do you think it happened?" a quiet voice asks me. "The last thing I can remember is going to sleep in my bed."

"I was running," I reply. "I stopped at a red light. That's all I've got."

She nods vacantly, deep-brown eyes staring off into the distance. I can tell by the look in them that she's not even contemplating escape. She's resigned to whatever happens to her next, and I want to shake her.

"I heard those women are being sold on some kind of slave planet. That's why they were taken away," she says.

"If we're landing, we have the chance to make a break for it. Did you see what the keys to this cell looked like?" I ask.

She tilts her head. "No."

She moves away from me like I'm contagious, as if being associated with me will lead to immediate unconsciousness and drooling on the floor.

I mean, she's not wrong.

I shake off that thought. I need to stay strong. Years ago, I read a book about survival. The book went into great detail about people who managed to survive. The trick is to be just hopeful enough to get through each day but not unrealistically optimistic. Too much optimism will lead to my hopes getting crushed if I can't immediately escape.

All I know is I refuse to end up wherever they're taking us next. If they've just unloaded a bunch of us to be sold as slaves and the Grivath who stunned me was pleased at the idea of me ending up in Durin, I have to do absolutely everything I can to *not* end up on that planet.

As if my thoughts conjured him, my favorite Grivath appears, with a wide smile just for me. He gestures to two other Grivath behind him, and I watch closely as one of them places his palm on a screen near the cage door and the lock clicks open.

Okay. So we just need to cut off a Grivath's hand so we can get out of this cage.

No problem.

I meet the Grivath's eyes as he bares his teeth. I refrain from flipping him off and instead vow it'll be his hand I use to get out of here.

I'm not a vengeful person by nature, but I'll sure enjoy cutting *his* hand off at the wrist.

Bowls of thick brown sludge are placed in front of us.

"Eat," one of the Grivath says, and women around fall on the gruel as if it's lobster. I'm guessing they've been awake and hungry for a lot longer than I have. I poke at it, trying not to gag as it wobbles like some kind of mix of porridge and Jell-O.

If I'm going to have any shot of getting out of here, I need to be separated from the rest of the prisoners. If I can, I'll come back and help them once I'm free. If I can't, then I guess I'll just have to live with it. As long as I get back to Brianna.

I pick up the bowl, considering. The Grivath who fired at me turns to leave, and I haul back my arm and let loose. My bowl hits the back of his head, showering him with sludge. It drips from his leathery gray shoulders down to the floor, flicking out and over anyone unfortunate enough to be nearby as he spins, roaring.

I'm not normally brave—just ask my father, who has

used my sick sister to keep me in line for twenty-five years. But I'll do whatever it takes to get back to Earth.

He storms toward me, and there's a stampede as women rush to get out of the way. The stick he shocked me with last time is in his hand, but I need to humiliate him enough to remove me from this cage.

"Oooh, big tough alien," I taunt as he gets closer. "Need a weapon to take on a tiny human?"

"That bitch be cray," a woman mutters as I stare him down.

He grins, showing off a wide set of fangs, rotted meat stuck between them.

"Wow, buddy, ever heard of a toothbrush?"

He takes a moment as the translator obviously does its work and then narrows his eyes in fury.

Within a couple of steps, he's close enough to touch, and he swings his arm to slap me across the face. I duck—more out of instinct than any skill—and he misses, to the sniggers of a few brave human women huddled near the back of the cage.

His gray face flushes darker, and he roars again, his open mouth giving me a whiff of Satan's toilet.

The Grivath follows up his swing with a backhand, and this time, I'm not fast enough to duck. It connects with enough power to throw me across the room.

Fire explodes across my face, and my eyes automatically prick with tears at the pain. I blink them back, push up to my knees, and call out as he turns to walk out of the cage.

"Hey, dickhead."

"Shiiiit, you think she's *trying* to make him kill her?"

He whirls, mouth falling open as if he can't quite believe I'm still talking. With the way my jaw feels, I can't believe it either.

"You hit like a fucking baby."

He storms toward me again as women gasp at my insanity, a few going as far as to cheer me on.

He picks me up by my arm and drags me out of the cage.

"Punishment," he says, and I gulp.

Sure, I'm getting out, but this Grivath may just be furious enough to kill me.

CHAPTER TWO

Amanda

I roll over, chains clanking.

The Grivath locked me up, ignoring my futile struggles. He grinned at me when he put me in this tiny cell and was raising his arm to hit me again when another Grivath opened the door.

"Do not break the merchandise," he ordered.

"I will be back," the first Grivath promised, and I actually shook in fear, wondering if his next hit would put me in the ground.

Except I'm nowhere near solid ground, and I can feel the hum of the ship beneath my cheek as I lie on the floor. Maybe they'll simply throw my body off the ship to join the space junk.

My plan backfired. Instead of having a greater chance of escape, I'm now locked up even tighter than the other human women. I should try to sleep and conserve my energy, but every time I close my eyes, I see my sister lying in a hospital bed, wondering where the hell I am.

Brianna has cystic fibrosis. Half the time you wouldn't know she's sick. The other half, she's so ill that you'd never expect her to get out of bed. But she does. Time and time again, she conquers the disease, refusing to let it take her down.

This time is different.

Bree was on the list for a lung transplant. We *all* breathed easier at the thought that the nightmare could be over. She'd still have CF, but she could leave her broken lungs in the past, like an old pair of shoes that no longer fit.

She had two dry runs. The first time, we rushed to the hospital only to be told it wasn't going to happen. The lungs weren't usable, and the devastation on Bree's face was excruciating.

But the simple, accepting nod she gave the last time she heard the news…that was much worse.

Two weeks ago, Bree got the flu. This progressed to pneumonia, which isn't unusual for her. But the last time I saw my sister, she was in the hospital, hooked up to a thousand machines, and talking about a living will.

I have to get out of here.

My stomach twists as I study the chains. I've never picked a lock in my life, and I'm fresh out of hairpins.

I jump, my heart beating like a drum as a loud, high-pitched siren cuts through the air. The world turns red as a light begins to flicker, and Grivath are sprinting past my cage. I haul myself to my feet, thankful my chains are at least long enough to do that. Something explodes somewhere, and I cry out as the ship rocks.

Unlike my sister, who's always been obsessed with space, I've found bliss in ignorance. This may be my first time on a spaceship, but I'm pretty sure it's not meant to be violently shuddering.

Are we going down?

I don't bother asking any of the Grivath about what's going on. That seems like a good way to earn more bruises. Instead, I crouch, sinking close to the bars of my cage, hoping to hear something useful.

"...attack...fleet...human slaves."

We're under attack? Or are the Grivath attacking another ship and that ship's fighting back?

From the panic I just glimpsed on one of the Grivath's faces, I'm assuming we're the ones being boarded.

Usually I'm an optimist. When your sister is as sick as mine is, your parents are assholes, and you haven't had a date in two years, you kinda have to believe things are going to get better.

Otherwise, you're not going to get out of bed in the morning.

But what are the chances a ship attacking the Grivath is going to be a good thing for the human women left?

Unless I can convince a Grivath to free me, I don't have a chance of getting out of here now.

The red lights continue to flicker, and the siren feels like ice picks stabbing into my brain. I make myself as small as possible, huddling into a ball as the ship shakes. There are fewer Grivath running past now, and it sounds like a war has broken out on the upper levels. I flinch at the screams and roars, wishing I were huddled with the other human women.

The battle goes on for what feels like hours. The ship is no longer shuddering, although I've heard two more explosions. My mind has fixated on the image of a giant hole in the side of this ship, sucking us all out to space.

Baking cookies in the fall. Trips to Annapolis in spring. Running the National Mall in the morning.

As much as I'd love the Grivath to die for what they've done to us, what if whoever is attacking is even worse? The Grivath are massive beasts, standing eight feet tall, with mouths full of large fangs. They also have those long weapons. I don't like the attackers' chances, although the sounds of the Grivath dying warm my heart.

Bree had insisted I go for a jog. I hadn't wanted to leave her side, but she knows that when life is at its hardest, my therapy is to run until my feet have blisters the size of walnuts. If I'd insisted on staying with her, I wouldn't have been out running. And I probably wouldn't have been taken.

I should've stayed with her. And then I wouldn't be about to die right now. I shake off that thought. The monsters howling and growling above me are solely to blame. How many lives have they ruined in the past few days?

Pounding feet sound on the stairs, and Grivath run past my cage again, this time retreating.

I chuckle when one of them trips in the chaos and face-plants. Then I do a little boogie when I realize it's the asshole who put me in this cage.

I may be about to die, but I'm gonna take my pleasure wherever I can find it.

He's flattened again as he tries to push to his knees, and every bone in my body wishes I could kick him while he's down. He lifts his head and sees me laughing.

Uh-oh.

He lets out a bellow and gets to his feet, elbowing another Grivath out of his way. Then he gives me a slow smile. I see my death between his teeth as he slaps his hairy hand against the palm reader and the cage door swings open.

Jaret

The battle was long and difficult. Nevertheless, we succeeded, taking control of the ship. Now we are rounding up the Grivath for execution. I am running operations from the control center in the heart of their ship while my men search for any Grivath who think to hide.

"Commander, we have found the human females. They are located in a cage under the dock." Usiv's tone is formal, but I tell he is shaken by the condition of the females.

"Are they healthy?"

"It is difficult to say at this point. There are twenty-two females. I suggest we transport them to the SSA *Horizon* in groups. I worry they may panic if they are let free before we move them."

I nod. "See that it is done." I move past Usiv, restless. My goal has been achieved, and the females are safe. So why do I feel as if I have more to do?

I make my way down to the human females, who are huddled in groups. Some of them are crying, and one of them stares at me with accusing eyes.

"Where will you take us?" she sobs.

I ignore her, moving on. My men can deal with any hysterics.

I stop as I come across the Grivath lieutenant's quarters. I killed him myself, and later, I plan to take some time to remember the look of horrified surprise on his face when he realized his life was over.

Like everything on this ship, the room is as sterile and gray as the Grivath themselves. I reach out and flip the sleeping platform, throwing a desk aside as an afterthought.

I do not know what I am looking for. No matter how many Grivath I kill, it will never be enough to satisfy my need for their blood.

They are the reason I grew up alone.

I ruthlessly bring myself under control, staring at the empty room in front of me. I do not feel satisfaction. I feel...nothing.

I spin, aimlessly wandering as my men prepare to disembark. We will lift anything useful from this ship, take all electronics for examination, and hopefully find some indication of how the Grivath managed to slip beneath our defenses and steal the human females.

"Commander?"

"Yes?"

"We damaged the hull in the battle. We have approximately two hours before this ship will be too compromised to fly."

The thought of another Grivath ship left devastated gives me a brief moment of pleasure.

"Have the human females been unloaded?"

"We are about halfway through. None of them have ever been off planet before and must be helped throughout the transport to our ship."

I nod absently and keep moving, prowling the Grivath ship for something I can use. Something that can help me destroy all of them. In the back of my mind, I'm well aware the Grivath wouldn't have left anything useful in case of this very event.

Screaming reaches my ears. The voice is high-pitched, full of terror, and something within me shifts uncomfortably. I clench my fists. The females were supposed to be kept together. Why are they screaming?

I make my way to the lower levels of the ship, sprinting as the screams turn to frightened shrieks.

The sound leads me to a small cage, the door wide open as a Grivath laughs at the human woman huddled and chained below him. He reaches out, slashing at her thin shirt, and she swings wildly at him.

I reach for my weapon, firing on full. He goes down, and I meet wide green eyes glazed with fear.

"You're an Arcav."

"You are observant."

I move back to the cage door, and she jerks at her chains.

"Don't you have a key for these?"

"My men will return to transport you off this ship shortly."

"Back to Earth?"

I ignore that question, and she makes a frustrated sound.

"At least let me out of the chains."

"I have had enough experience with human females to know that the only way you will stay where I keep you is if you are unable to move."

I frown as I think of our queen. She has taught me all I need to know about deceptive humans.

The human female's mouth drops open as I turn to leave, and I have a sudden, unexpected urge to stroke her full bottom lip.

"You psycho! Don't leave me here!"

I shut the cell door behind me, ignoring her shouted curses.

Amanda

I slump back, exhausted. That Arcav had the coldest eyes I've ever seen. I've stared into eyes like that almost every day of my life, and I would bet he's just as much of a sociopath as my father.

Broken people have eyes like that. And they break everyone else around them too.

Case in point: He left me in here with a dead body. I eye the Grivath in disgust. Sure, I'm glad he's dead, but I would've much preferred to have been the one to pull the trigger before hightailing it away from his bleeding corpse.

My wrists are already raw and oozing blood from my useless attempts to get free. The bastard could've at least let me out of the chains. I sigh. All I can do is wait. The good news? While the Arcav aren't my favorite people, at least they're the devils I know. They don't kill indiscriminately, and they need human women too much to sell us off as slaves.

I feel like a weight has been lifted off my shoulders for the first time since I woke up. The Arcav travel between Arcavia and Earth all the time. They may not look much like white knights, with their lethal horns and bulging muscles, but as far as I'm concerned, they're my guardian angels.

"I'm coming, Bree. Just hold on."

I'm dizzy with relief, and my body has hit a wall. I curl up against the side of my cage, as far from the Grivath's body as I can, and fall fast asleep.

I'm sitting on my bed, showing Bree my newest element while she uses her nebulizer. I've been collecting them for a year now, desperate to get my hands on as many as I can. A few months ago, I began assigning elements to everyone we know. When Bree asked me which element she was, I told her I needed some time to decide, and now I've made my choice.

She leans over, coughing, and I pound her back, helping to dislodge some of the mucus that makes her life so difficult.

"Thanks." She leans back, holding out her hand.

I place it gently on her palm. "This is carbon. I know it doesn't look like much. But it's the most important element for life."

I lean closer until our foreheads are pressed together as we study the pencil lead I've crushed and collected in my tiny container.

"Did you know that carbon also becomes diamonds? They're the hardest known substance on Earth."

I examine my sister's pale face as she stares at the carbon. Diamonds can withstand a lot. But once the temperature gets hot enough, they burn up, turning into carbon dioxide.

Sometimes my stomach twists when I think about how sick Brianna is. We were born seven minutes apart. But some cosmic joke gave her a chronic disease, while I'm healthy as a horse.

"You've got that look on your face again," she says.

"Sorry."

Bree hates it when I wallow. She sometimes says I take her CF worse than she does.

I startle awake, looking up into the eyes of another Arcav. This one is wearing some kind of uniform, and his expression looks briefly pained when he takes in my chains and the dead Grivath in my cell.

"I am sorry you were left here."

"Not your fault. I'm guessing that guy is your boss?"

He nods and presses something on the palm scanner, and the door swings open. The Arcav have obviously completely overridden everything on this ship, and I smile in satisfaction. Humans may be huddled near the bottom of this galaxy's food chain, but right now it looks like the Grivath aren't up all that high either.

"My name is Velax," he says, producing a key and unlocking my cuffs.

"I'm Amanda."

Velax's brow lowers when he sees the state of my wrists, and he winces as his gaze scans my face. I have no doubt I have some pretty impressive bruises thanks to the Grivath. He offers me his hand, helping me as I move stiffly to my feet. Then he pauses, finally leaning forward and lifting me over the dead Grivath before immediately releasing me.

"Where are the other women?"

"They have almost all been transported to our ship. If you come with me, I will take you there now."

Well, I'm sure not going to hang around on this ship. I follow Velax out, my head pounding as I glance around me, taking everything in. This ship is sterile, cold, and reminds me of an old bunker. It's freezing, and I shiver as Velax leads me down to the ship's dock, ignoring the Grivath bodies lying at every turn. I feel a brief pang of sympathy as I pass a Grivath sprawled near the dock, outstretched arm reaching for a weapon inches away. I couldn't care less for these Grivath, but I wonder if they have families. Will they get closure? Or will this ship never be found?

A touch at my elbow pulls me from my thoughts, and Velax gestures toward a ship. A few women are already boarding, although others are hesitating as they eye it nervously.

"This pod will take you to our ship—the SSA *Horizon*," Velax says, and I nod, blowing out a breath. My neck prickles, and I turn, making eye contact with the Arcav with the dead eyes. I narrow my own eyes automatically, and he scans my body before turning away dismissively.

"Who is he?" I ask Velax.

"That's Jaret, the commander. He is in control of the entire Arcav armed forces."

"The entire armed forces? What's he doing on this ship?"

Velax lifts one shoulder in a shrug, and I stare at the gesture, so human and yet so alien at the same time. Bree would choke on her own spit if she knew I was talking to an Arcav right now.

I love you, Bree. Just keep breathing.

"No one is quite sure why. This is where I leave you. Healers will take care of your injuries on the ship, and I will check on you later."

I offer him a smile, and he grins back, suddenly looking young and boyish. I feel icy eyes on me again and barely restrain from flipping them off.

CHAPTER THREE

Amanda

The trip in the pod is incredible, and I'm itching for a camera. Bree would be wriggling with excitement if she were here, enveloped by the dark blanket of space.

Whenever I imagined outer space, which truthfully, wasn't often, I pictured it as cold, black, and empty.

I couldn't have been more wrong.

Five of us human women sit in awed silence as we take in the vast stretch of darkness broken by the glow of brightly colored planets.

Space isn't empty. It's infinite. Mysterious. Breathtaking.

A few years ago, I went scuba diving in Mexico. I've never been able to quiet my mind, but slowly floating under the water, surrounded by fish and sea creatures, was the closest I've ever come to meditation.

This trip is like that.

Within a couple of minutes, we're close to the Arcav ship, and I wish I could float through space for just a little longer.

The SSA *Horizon* is shaped like an hourglass. As we get closer, I can see the gigantic, cylindrical dock. A massive door begins to open, and our pod flies inside, pulling into what must essentially be a space garage. The door immediately closes behind us, and the Arcav driver directs the pod through another door and into a parking slot.

We're assisted out of the pod, all of us huddling together like frightened sheep. Another Arcav appears, this one even taller than any of the others I've seen, his horns straightening as he stares at us for a moment before blinking his glowing eyes.

"Welcome to the SSA *Horizon*," he says. "The other human females are currently eating. Please follow me."

He turns, and I position myself at the back of our little flock so I'll have more time to linger and stare.

The difference between the Grivath ship and the Arcav ship is stark. The Grivath ship was no-frills military, while the Arcav ship is lush, packed wall to wall with comfortable furniture and even real flowers in vases on the tables. We're directed down long corridors, up flights of stairs, through cozy sitting rooms, and finally into a large dining room, where the other women have congregated.

Each of them looks dazed and shocked, and I'm sure I look just the same. We sit while a woman with six arms and pale-yellow skin places food in front of us.

"Is that...steak?"

The woman smiles. "The Arcav were sent on a mission to rescue you, so they ensured the ship was stocked with human food. Please let us know if there is anything else you would like."

She leaves us eating, and we begin introductions. Most of the other women were taken in their sleep, although a few of us seem to have been plucked off the street—maybe even as an afterthought.

"Anyone know how long we've been gone for?" I ask.

"I'm guessing less than a week," a woman who introduced herself as Maggie answers. "We all kind of woke up at different times. I don't know what they did to us..." She trails off, and we all shudder.

I dig in to a cheeseburger and fries, barely keeping my eyes open. I can't afford to fall asleep before I talk to whoever is in charge. My stomach churns, and I put my burger down. It's likely the top dog is the commander with the blank, disinterested stare. I'm going to need to talk to him and find out how quickly I can get back to Earth.

The rest of the human women arrive, and we compare stories. We're from all over the United States, Central America, and Canada. None of us can remember being taken, and all of us are in that stupefied part of shock, where your arm has red marks from constant pinching to see if you're awake or trapped in a nightmare.

The commander doesn't show, and those of us who are injured are taken to what Velax calls a medi-center to be fixed up. I've heard rumors of Arcav technology, particularly in the medical field, and my mouth drops open as an Arcav runs some kind of electronic stick along the skin at my wrists and it begins to knit back together.

"Gross," I whisper. "But so cool."

My head is next, and I feel a flash of pain as the Arcav heals the deep bruising.

"Can this heal deeper things? Like, say, a pair of seriously low-functioning lungs?"

The Arcav raises his brow and tucks the stick away. "No."

All righty then.

We're taken to our rooms, which are small but immaculate and comfortable. Some of the women choose to bunk together, but I'm more interested in privacy.

The plush bed tempts me, but I take a shower and then pace to keep myself awake. Once the lights have automatically dimmed, I slip out of the room and trace my steps back toward the dining room. It's empty, so I keep moving, slinking in and out of rooms as I search for someone who can tell me what's going on.

I hear voices and creep closer, finding the commander—Jaret, I correct myself—in a room with a group of Arcav. They're sitting around a table, a few of them eating, while they talk to an Arcav on a large screen. I freeze and begin to back further away, when I bump my elbow into the door.

Heads immediately turn, and I feel heat creeping up my neck. I lock eyes with Jaret, and his widen briefly with surprise before he gets to his feet.

"What are you doing here?"

"I need to talk to you."

His face darkens, and he gestures to Velax, who immediately rises, obviously about to escort me back to my room.

"Wait a second. You can't just haul us around without giving us any information. Where are you taking us?"

Those cold eyes stare at me, something dark moving in them as Velax takes my elbow, ready to haul me away.

"We will go back to Arcavia."

"What?" My voice is high, and I shake off Velax's hand. "I can't go to Arcavia. I need to get back to Earth!"

"Both this ship and I are needed on Arcavia. Once we have landed, any human women who wish to return to Earth will be taken back on a shuttle, provided they are not mates."

My mouth drops open, and I gape like a fish. "I'm not going to Arcavia."

Jaret looks like he's coming perilously close to rolling his eyes.

"I beg to differ." He nods at Velax, who takes my arm again, this time not allowing me to shake him off.

"Please," I say, but Jaret has already turned away, speaking with the Arcav on the screen, who has a smile dancing around his mouth.

They think this is a joke. That I'm just some hysterical human female who'll be inconvenienced by the extra time spent away from Earth.

I follow Velax, completely numb. He tries to make conversation but falls silent when his eyes take in my face.

"I am sorry you are upset," he says as we reach my room. "I am sure you will be back on Earth within a couple of weeks."

"I don't have a couple of weeks," I whisper, closing the door behind me.

Jaret

I attempt to continue my meeting with Methi, but my mind keeps returning to the devastation on the human female's face.

I have no choice. Varian has ordered the ship and his commander back to Arcavia, so that is where we will be going. These human females must learn that the entire galaxy will not bow down to their wishes.

When Varian was courting his mate, he made concessions that will impact the Arcav for the rest of our days.

Our very survival depends on taking human mates, thanks to Korva's treachery. When he poisoned our water, he ensured Arcav females would no longer be born. He then mutated the humans' DNA so that we would not just have to mate with humans but would need to take them back to Arcavia to receive the Alni plant in order for them to be as long-lived as our race.

Harlow, Varian's mate, has managed to convince Varian to allow Korva to rejoin society. According to her, all the crazed Arcav males need is to spend time with human females. Her theory is this will allow the Arcav to go for longer without finding their mates—lowering the risk of insanity. It should also give those who have lost their mates the chance to have some form of a life, without needing to be removed from society.

I would not have believed Korva's release possible if I had not heard the news directly from Varian himself. Apparently, Korva is still slowly recovering, relearning to speak and spending most of his time alone. He now has a life again, although I doubt our race will ever recover from the damage he has inflicted. He is a traitor of the worst kind. One who has forced us to mate with humans, a backward, short-lived race who imagined themselves alone in this galaxy before we invaded.

I snort, and Methi pauses, raising an eyebrow.

"I apologize," I say. "It has been a long day. We will continue this tomorrow morning."

He nods, and I turn off the ComScreen, noting Velax has returned. I did not miss the interest in his gaze when he stared at the human female, so belligerent as she insisted on returning to Earth.

Truthfully, humans are unremarkable compared to Arcav. They are short in stature, fine-boned, and have neither horns nor claws. They are weak, easily killed, and slowly destroying their planet and one another with battles, wars, and pollution.

Unfortunately, my mind continues to return to the female who dared to raise her voice to me. She is tall for a human, although much shorter than any Arcav. Her long hair is light, falling down her back in a smooth sheet. She has the tiniest dots across her small nose, as if she has been speckled with paint. And her eyes...they were amber, long-lidded, and fierce as she glared at me.

I feel my body harden and make a mental note to schedule a visit to Brexa. She owes me information, and I intend to collect.

CHAPTER FOUR

Amanda

The next morning, I lie awake in bed, stewing. I've slept for a few hours, but my dreams haunt me. In them, my sister gasps desperately for air, calling my name again and again.

I know I should get some more sleep so I can be at my best today. I need to somehow get off this ship and back to Earth. My hands fist as I picture the dismissal in Jaret's eyes. If he won't help me, I'll get back to Earth myself.

I take slow breaths and run through the periodic table to calm down.

I'm an element geek. There, I admit it.

Everything on Earth is made up of 118 elements. I have no great interest in chemistry, or any science really, but the idea there are only 118 building blocks that created everything?

Fascinating.

I started collecting when I was small, finding elements wherever I could. Eventually, my focus shifted to boys and friends. But I never lost my curiosity and interest in the elements. Each one is unique, adding or removing something in the world.

It's hydrogen that makes the stars shine. Earth's sun consumes 600 million tons of hydrogen every second. It converts that hydrogen into 596 million tons of helium. The other four million tons every second? They're converted into energy.

A tiny amount of this energy makes it back to Earth. Once it reaches us, it becomes the glow of a winter's dawn, or the lingering warmth of a long summer afternoon.

Seventy-five percent of the universe is hydrogen. It's everywhere, but we never think about it.

Jaret's blank face dances through my mind, and I scowl. If he were an element, he'd be nitrogen. Liquid nitrogen is so cold that it can freeze almost anything. I smile. Once something is frozen with liquid nitrogen, it can be shattered with little more than a thought.

I unclench my fists at a knock on the door. "Come in."

It's Maggie, who enters with a tentative smile. "How are you today?"

"They say they're taking us to Arcavia."

Her face pales, and she sits on the end of my bed. It's made of some kind of gel, and she sinks down a few inches as it shapes itself to her butt.

"What?"

"Yeah. If we're not mates, we get to go home within a few weeks," I say bitterly, and her face clears.

"I've taken the test. I'm not a mate." A flash of regret crosses her face. "At least we'll get to explore a new planet, right? Maybe we can see this as some kind of adventure."

"I need to get back to Earth."

"Why—oh. Your sister." Her face falls. "I'm so sorry, Amanda. This couldn't have happened at a worse time."

There isn't a good time to be abducted by aliens, but she's right. If Bree had been healthy right now, maybe I also would've been able to see this experience as a big adventure.

I swing my legs over the side of my bed, and Maggie gets to her feet.

"They have a whole room of human clothes for us to choose from," she says. "Let me show you."

The room could give a clothing store on Earth a run for its money. I stare at rack after rack of jeans, shorts, shirts, and dresses in a variety of sizes and finally pull out a long, heavily patterned maxi dress. Maybe the bright colors will cheer me up.

"Let's go get something to eat," I suggest.

Truthfully, I'm not interested in food. I'm interested in mapping every part of this ship until I can figure out a way to get off it.

The Arcav who drove our pod didn't seem to be driving so much as steering. Most of the time, he spoke to the computer controlling it, and it responded accordingly.

If I can get back to the dock, maybe I can find a pod and take it back to Earth.

Distantly, I realize this is a bad plan. It's my first time in space, I've never even flown a plane, and I have no idea how to actually get back to Earth. But logic has no place here right now.

Cystic fibrosis is no longer a death sentence that guarantees a short, painful life. These days, many people live into their thirties, forties, even fifties if they manage their health well. But Bree has always had bad luck. Her whole life, it's been one thing after another for her. Lung infection after lung infection.

When we were growing up, I knew deep in my bones that sometimes, the only reason Bree pulled through was because she refused to leave me with our parents.

She lived for me. If I have to, I'll risk dying to get back to her.

I follow Maggie to the dining room. From what I understand so far, this part of the ship is the living quarters. The ship is multilevel, with long corridors leading to the control center. Guards are posted at various points, but unlike the Grivath's ship, it doesn't feel like a military base. There's a focus on comfort, with soft-colored walls and thick rugs in the living quarters. If I didn't look out the window, I could almost forget I'm currently hurtling through space.

I eat a few bites of some kind of porridge, tuning out the other women as I strategize. I startle at a touch on my shoulder, and the table goes silent as we look up at Velax. He has kind eyes and a ready smile, which creases his cheek as he grins down at me.

"How are you today?" he asks, his voice low, ignoring the whispers from my table.

"Uh, I'm okay. I was actually wondering if you could help me with something. I was looking for a pen and a piece of paper to write down my thoughts. But I can't seem to find anything."

Velax raises an eyebrow. "We do not use paper very often," he says, and my shoulders slump. "However, I believe I can help."

He pulls out a small tablet from his pocket and offers it to me.

"You may use this," he says, also handing me a stylus, and I smile for the first time since I woke up on the Grivath ship.

"Thank you," I say, and he grins again.

"You are welcome." He raises his eyes to the other women at my table. "Please do not hesitate to ask if you need anything else."

He walks away, and a woman named Amy snorts as we watch him leave. "He'd sure like to help you with *anything* you need, if you get me."

The other women crack up, and despite myself, I grin.

After breakfast, we make our way to one of the sitting rooms, where everyone hangs out in small groups, drinking coffee. One of the women is sitting alone in a corner, and I make my way over, also hoping for some privacy.

"Hi," I say. "I'm Amanda."

Sad blue eyes meet mine. "I'm Veronica," she says in heavily accented English.

"Are you okay?"

She slowly shakes her head. "I heard from Maggie we are going to Arcavia." Her eyes fill with tears. "I have two children who are waiting for me in Guatemala. I cannot take the time to go to Arcavia and then back to Earth."

I grind my teeth. I've never had a problem with the Arcav except when it comes to their complete disregard for humans' wants and needs. I took my blood test, and as far as I know, it's still being processed. I didn't whine or complain or focus on things I couldn't control. All I cared about was being left alone to live my life.

Now I've had an inside look into exactly how powerful the Arcav are and how little our preferences mean to them. What if Veronica ends up being a mate? Will she be forced to stay in Arcavia, hoping the Arcav will bring her kids to her?

"Listen," I whisper. "I'm going to get back to Earth. Do you want to come with me?"

She wipes at a tear, staring at me. "How?"

"I'm not sure yet, but I'm not going to just sit around and let these guys haul me off to Arcavia. You think you can help me make a map of this ship?"

She nods. "I am an architect in Guatemala. I will help you draw."

An architect. Perfect. I hand the tablet over. Other than the trip to and from her room, Veronica hasn't seen much of the ship. So I tell her what I've seen, and she draws an outline of the ship, filling in what we know so far.

"Do you know how to get back to the dock?" I ask.

She shakes her head and leans closer, pointing to the middle of the hourglass and then the very top. "The command or control center is likely to be either here or here. We know the dock is at the other end, in the widest part."

"Where do you think we are now?"

She shrugs. "I think there are at least six floors."

"Okay. How about we go take a walk? We should probably get some exercise, don't you think?"

Veronica grins. "Exercise is important."

Jaret

I am not a good man.

Everything I do, every step I take, is with one goal in mind: strengthen the Arcav and eventually annihilate the Grivath.

The female with the amber eyes plays on my thoughts. If I were the type of male to have empathy for those weaker than me, the accusation in those eyes would sting.

Centuries ago, the Arcav's need to mate was considered a

blessing. The gods had chosen one perfect soul to complete us. We felt superior to those races who would never know the joy of being mated.

When I was just a few years old, I realized how wrong we were.

I am shaken from my thoughts as Varian's face appears on the ComScreen.

"I have spoken to the Fecax. They are working on a shield with sensors that will alert us if the Grivath get too close to Earth."

We recently discovered the Grivath have managed to access Fecax technology, allowing them to use shielding to render their ships invisible. This is likely how they were able to take the human females. They are unaware we can detect their shielding, and I bare my teeth in satisfaction. The Grivath will send more ships to Earth, looking for human females to sell. When they do, we will destroy them.

"Any news about the Fecax princess?

"No. I am thinking of sending Methi to Fecax with Talis. I will wait until I hear back from Xiax before I make the decision."

Methi is a good choice. He is young, but his easy confidence and good-natured personality make it easy for him to convince people to tell him things they would otherwise not mention.

"And Harlow?" I ask.

Methi is her favorite and is usually assigned to be one of her guards when she is separated from Varian during the day.

Varian's face lightens, his shoulders straighten, and he grins.

"We are having a child," he says proudly. Even through

the screen, his happiness radiates from him. The next generation of Arcav royalty will be born.

"Congratulations."

"Thank you." He nods. "Harlow is currently unwell during most of the day." His face darkens. "The healers say this is normal for human women. But I will not be leaving her side until she is no longer unwell. The sooner you get back, the better."

We say our goodbyes, and I walk in the direction of my rooms. A soft, welcoming scent reaches me, and I swing my head, watching as Amanda and another female walk toward me. Her dress is an assault on my eyes, patterned with every color of the rainbow.

"What are you doing down here?" I growl.

Her entire body screams defiance. "Going for a walk. We need some exercise," she says, slipping a tablet into her pocket. "Is that okay with you, Commander?"

Her sarcasm slides right off me, and I focus on the other human.

"Is that what you are doing?" I ask her, and she meets my eyes.

"Of course."

"You should not be on this floor without an escort. You may walk in the human quarters and the entire third floor."

"Why?"

I pause, unused to being questioned by anyone. Amanda stares at me, her gaze unwavering.

Because you make me lose my focus. Because you remind me of my mother. And because you make me long for a female of my own.

"Because this is what I have decided."

She wrinkles her small nose in disgust at my reply, and I study her for a long moment.

"Leave," I tell the other female, who nods, striding away rapidly.

"Don't talk to her like that! What's the matter with you?"

I back her against the wall, staring down at her.

"You have dots on your face," I murmur.

She frowns, and then her eyebrow lifts. "You mean freckles?"

"Freckles." I taste the word. It does not seem enough to describe the scatter of dots that highlight her smooth creamy skin. A faint flush has reached her cheeks, and I ignore the almost uncontrollable urge to sweep her dress aside and see where else she is pink.

"I am watching you, little one. Do not think to push me."

She stares at me and then slams her hands against my chest, demanding freedom.

I move away as her small fists clench and a pulse pounds in her neck. I want to lick it.

"Maybe," she hisses as she turns, "you shouldn't push me."

CHAPTER FIVE

Amanda

I don't think I've ever met anyone as cold, arrogant, and controlling as the Arcav commander. My father's face flashes before my eyes, and I snort. Okay, maybe one other person.

I find Veronica in her bedroom, and we put our heads together, adding as much information as we can to our recreation of the ship.

"This looks fine," I finally say. "We don't need the whole ship, just the key parts so we know how to get back to the dock and which areas to avoid."

Veronica nods and puts down the tablet.

"Okay," she says. "What's next?"

"As much as I'd love to just haul ass to the dock and try to steal a pod, we need to be strategic. We can't risk getting caught. Let's watch the Arcav tonight and note where they are and what their security looks like. The Arcav are definitely keeping an eye on me, so maybe you can sneak down to the dock and check it out. Or at least get close," I say as her face pales.

Veronica squares her shoulders. "Of course. I will do whatever it takes."

That's what love does to us. When you truly love someone, you're willing to do anything to be by their side. Something tells me the commander hasn't yet discovered this universal truth. I doubt he's ever loved anyone at all.

We retire to our separate rooms to take naps, since we'll be up all night. But I'm still groggy when we meet the other women for dinner.

"What do you think Arcavia is like?" one of them asks me.

I shrug. I'm not going to Arcavia, so I couldn't care less.

"Probably pretty," I finally say when she stares at me expectantly. "These guys have basically shut down anything that can contribute to climate change on Earth. Something tells me their planet is pristine."

Before the Arcav invaded, I was working in DC, writing policy and white papers for a think tank. Most of my work was centered around increasing bike lanes and public transport options in cities throughout the United States. Once the invasion happened, we were all laid off as government officials fled, and whole cities became ghost towns. Within a few months, people began moving back once they realized the Arcav didn't plan to completely level our major cities.

Humans are remarkably resilient. We can get used to almost anything. Watching the Arcav announce the names of human women who would be mated with the Arcav became the new normal. We gritted our teeth when the Arcav enforced laws that prevented humans from owning weapons. And we shrugged when they banned fossil fuels, replacing them with clean Arcav technology. Six months later, it was almost as if the Arcav had always been there. Unless, of course, a woman was unfortunate or fortunate enough to be a mate, depending on how they felt about it.

I spend the evening hanging out with the human women, encouraging them to explore the ship. We walk in groups, and I subtly urge them along the route that Veronica and I are hoping to take. We're planning to escape around this time tomorrow night, and I mentally note where the guards are at each point of our walk, and especially when they change shifts.

"I'm tired," Maggie says. "I'm going to head back to my room."

The others quickly agree, and I hesitate. "I'm going to wander for a little longer."

Maggie frowns at me, likely taking in the purple shadows under my eyes, but hugs me good night, yawning as she walks off.

"Psssst, Amanda!"

I turn, taking in Veronica's pale face. "What's wrong?"

She rushes toward me, hands shaking as she reaches me. "There's no one in the dock right now. There has been some sort of emergency, and everyone rushed out. If we're going to go, we should take the opportunity."

I'm instantly trembling with adrenaline, a drop of sweat sliding down my lower back. This is it. We're unlikely to get a better chance than this.

"Okay. Let's go."

We sprint to the dock, running through empty halls and downstairs to the lower floors. At one point, we freeze as an Arcav hurries down the corridor, thankfully in the opposite direction. By the time we enter the dock, we're clutching at each other like children, inching forward with our eyes scanning for any signs of movement.

"I have a suggestion." Veronica's voice is low and shaky. She's pale, her face covered in sweat, and I'm sure I look the same.

"What's up?"

"I don't know how far the pods can travel, but I think it's unlikely they'll make it all the way to Earth. Otherwise, we would've seen the Arcav arriving in them."

She makes a good point. I've seen the Arcav ships on TV, and while they're not as large as the behemoth we're standing in right now, they're definitely much, much bigger than the pods.

"You're right." My stomach sinks as we stare at the pod we planned to take. Am I just kidding myself? There are bad ideas, and then there are suicidal ones.

Veronica is trembling beside me, but she grabs my hand, pulling me to a part of the dock I hadn't seen.

"Look," she says, and I grin.

"It looks almost exactly like the ship the Arcav queen boarded when she left Earth," I say. Her coronation was televised around the world, and I don't know a single person who didn't watch it.

"I know."

"Okay, this is a much better option. Now how the hell do we get inside it?"

Our translators allow us to understand languages like Arcav—and apparently also other languages from races like the Grivath—but they definitely don't help us when it comes to reading them. We climb under the ship, searching each panel until Veronica finally finds a small button. A side door on the ship opens, and a staircase slowly lowers until it hits the ground. The ship doesn't quite roll out a red carpet, but it's close.

We look at each other.

"Are you sure you want to do this?" I ask.

We both know the chances of this escape attempt having a happy ending are low.

Veronica brushes a tear from her face impatiently. "My kids have no one. My father is a drunk, my mother just died, and my siblings all live in the States. My only hope is my maid has found my babies and has been kind enough to look after them. I *have* to get back to them. We can do this, Manda. I know we can."

My heart clenches. That's Bree's nickname for me.

"Okay. Let's go."

We climb the stairs, and I leave Veronica to figure out how to pull them up behind us and close the door. I make my way to the control center, and my heart sinks as I stare at thousands of buttons, all labeled in a foreign language.

"If only this thing had autopilot," I mutter.

"Language detected."

The voice is smooth, sultry, and female, seemingly coming from midair, and I whirl, heart pounding.

"Human. English. Would you like to engage autopilot?"

"You've got to be fucking kidding."

"You would like a joke?"

"No, no," I say, planting myself in what appears to be the captain's seat. "Can I use autopilot to get us out of here?"

"Yes. Would you like to engage autopilot?"

"Hell yeah. Engage autopilot."

Veronica appears, and I can tell she's holding on by a thread.

"I can't pull up the stairs and close the door."

"Uh, computer," I say, "Can you close the door?"

"Closing entrance."

"Dios mío," Veronica says, blowing out a breath. "We're getting out of here."

I grin. "I feel kinda bad. Do you think we should have told the other women?"

She shakes her head. "They were all excited to go to Arcavia. You and I are the only ones who need to get back immediately."

"Autopilot engaged."

"Okay, great. Um, can you open the main door?"

"Request denied."

"Why?"

"Request has been overridden."

"Overridden by who?" I demand.

Veronica curses beside me, grabs my arm, and points below us, where Jaret is standing, surrounded by other Arcav males. We stare at each other silently, his expression bored, my body shaking in rage.

Then he holds up a tablet identical to the one currently in my pocket.

Our sketch of the ship is evident, even from up this high. My gaze shifts to Velax, who's currently standing behind Jaret. He looks miserable, guilt written all over his face, and as soon as he meets my eyes, he turns away.

Jaret gestures toward the ground next to him, indicating we should get off the ship.

I raise my hand in a gesture of my own, and Veronica lets out a choked laugh even as tears stream down her cheeks.

"Computer?"

"Yes?"

"Can you override Jaret's command?"

"Commander Jaret has full authority over all military vehicles according to section 8, subsection 32..."

"Forget it."

Veronica turns her back on Jaret, and I do the same. We slump down, hiding on the floor like kids, neither of us willing to actually get off the ship. This was the only plan I had. I'm all out of ideas.

"I really thought we could do it," she says.

"Yeah. That son of a bitch set us up."

I can't even work up a good rage. Instead, I can feel myself sinking into depression, and I curl up on the ground. Let him come and drag us off.

Jaret

Never have I met a female so infuriating. I knew the moment the human began planning her escape. In response, I arranged for my men to leave their posts so we could get this unfortunate scene over with.

It took two of my men to drag her off the ship, kicking and screaming the entire time. I do not believe I have ever seen Velax look so uncomfortable, his head hung low and his brow furrowed as he watched my men enter the ship.

The other female went quietly, although her shattered sobs caused more than a few furrowed brows amongst my men.

I pinch my nose, attempting to relieve a pounding headache. I do not have time to go to the healer. I am also well aware the cause of my pain is the female who was just carried past as she pointed one small, trembling finger at my face, voice shaking as she vowed to *end* me.

I have ordered for her to be taken to the small cells on the lowest level of the ship. I do not want to have to keep her there for long. Arcav do not believe in torturing females. However, if she cannot be convinced to end this way of thinking, she will be staying there for the rest of this trip.

Something shifts uncomfortably inside me as I imagine her curled up on the cold floor, tears streaking her face.

It is as if Amanda is a magnet. I cannot help but make my way down to where she is lying, just as I had pictured her, curled up on the floor. She is no longer crying though, simply staring at the cold bars that separate us. Seeing her out of reach, behind cold metal, makes my horns straighten, and my voice comes out harsh.

"What were you thinking?"

She ignores me, although I am paying close enough attention that I notice her eyes narrowing fractionally at my question.

"Why do you insist on acting this way? You will be returned to Earth within two weeks."

"I don't *have* two weeks, you arrogant asshole," she says, and although her tone cuts like a blade, I relax slightly at the sound of her voice.

"Why? What is so important that you must get back to Earth so quickly? Is it a lover?"

My claws extend without warning, and I lift one hand, frowning down at it.

"No. As I tried to tell you multiple times, my sister is really sick. If I don't get back in time, it's possible she could die, and I won't be there." Her voice hitches. "Even though I swore if it ever came to that, I'd never leave her side."

She bursts into tears, and I feel as if my chest is being crushed. It is not that I do not sympathize. I know what other Arcav say, but I am not an unfeeling monster. I can only imagine the devastation if I were able to see my mother, to give her some form of support during her final moments, only to have that chance ripped from me without warning.

"If I speak to the Arcav king and ask to switch flight

paths, will you cease your attempts to escape?" It is unlikely Varian will agree, and the thought saddens me. I need to ensure this human understands the stupidity of her actions.

She is silent, and I continue, hoping to get through to her.

"It takes years to learn how to navigate space. You would have doomed both yourself and the other human woman with you." I am growling at the thought, and I wonder if I resemble a beast to her. It is the first time I have ever attempted to determine the thoughts of a human.

She sits up, wiping her nose with her hand. Her skin is pale, her hands dirty, and red blotches stand out starkly on her face. For some reason, I still find her compelling, even in her distressed state.

I make another mental note to schedule a dinner with Brexa.

"Will you behave if I allow you to leave this cell?"

"When will you talk to Varian?"

I sigh. "It is the middle of the night in Arcavia, and I believe the conversation will go much more smoothly if I speak with him in the morning."

She gets to her feet, then nods to me as if she is a queen and I am her servant.

"Let me out, then."

CHAPTER SIX

Amanda

I wake early the next day, my stomach churning and neck muscles tense as I get ready to find Jaret. Last night I was separated from Veronica and given a new bedroom close to Jaret's quarters so he can keep an eye on me.

The bedroom is an upgrade, but I can't appreciate the extra space and furniture. I make my way to Jaret's quarters and knock on the door.

He opens it, a frown on his face and a towel wrapped around his waist. I struggle to keep my mouth from dropping open as I take in his abs and chest. The guy is built like a tank. He turns away from me, moving further into the room, and my tongue practically hangs out of my mouth as I check out his huge shoulders and sleek back muscles.

He disappears into his bathroom, and I hesitate, realizing he still hasn't said anything.

"Uh...Jaret?"

"Yes?"

"Have you talked to Varian yet?"

"No. It is still too early in Arcavia."

I feel my shoulders slump, and they lower even more when he returns from the bathroom fully dressed.

"Listen, I truly appreciate you guys saving us from the Grivath. But what about the women who were unloaded on the first planet? What will happen to them?"

"We left men in Gule who are tracking the human females." He shifts. "Gule is a slave planet. We will do everything we can to find them and return them to Earth."

I blow out a breath. I can't stop thinking about Charlie. She was what my grandma would call a firecracker, and I hate the thought of her and the other women sold as slaves.

"I have been thinking."

"Uh-huh?"

"We have the ability to speak with humans on Earth. If you like, you can call your sister and speak with her."

"Oh my God!"

Why didn't I think of that? I can tell her I didn't just leave her with no warning and I'll be there soon.

"I would love to. Wow, this is amazing."

I'm beaming, and I dance in place at the thought of talking to Bree. Jaret's cold eyes scan me, widening slightly as if I'm insane, but even he can't ruin my mood. He didn't need to offer this call—our deal was only for him to talk to Varian. Maybe he's a half-decent guy under it all.

He takes a step closer, eyes on mine, and I have the weirdest feeling he's somehow inhaling my joy like a vampire who has no ability to feel it himself.

"You should prepare yourself," he says coldly. "It is unlikely Varian will agree to allow this ship to go to Earth. This may be the last time you speak with your sister."

Tears are dripping down my cheeks before he's even

finished speaking, and his face softens slightly as he steps even closer.

"How is it that you feel so much?" he asks me, reaching up a hand.

I freeze, unable or unwilling to move a muscle as his palm cups my jaw. I imagined he would feel as cold as a corpse, but his heated skin tells me he's very much alive.

"How is it that you don't?"

The ghost of a smile crosses his lips, and I stare, fascinated.

"Come. You will talk to your sister."

He opens another door off his bedroom, which leads into a small sitting room. From there, yet another door opens into a meeting room, which holds a large screen.

Another Arcav appears, introducing himself as Zarbi. He gets down to business, flicking on the screen and then turning to me.

"What is the contact number?"

I blank. I don't have anyone's number memorized. My hands sweat and panic, and I turn to Jaret, who steps closer.

"If you do not have the number, we will find it." He looks at Zarbi, who gulps and immediately nods.

"Of course. Just tell me her name and where she is located."

I rattle off the information, and a few seconds later, the phone begins to ring.

I stand, my heart pounding as I urge her to pick up.

Zarbi tries three times, and each time we get her voicemail. Finally, I leave a frantic message.

"Bree, it's me. I'm coming back to you, I promise." I avoid Jaret's eyes. I *will* get back to her. "Just hold on, okay? I love you."

I'm trembling, black spots in front of eyes. What if she's

dead? What if, when I got abducted by fucking aliens, Bree died, wondering where her little sister was?

"You will sit down immediately." Jaret's icy voice interrupts the deluge of my thoughts as he takes my arm, pushing me into a chair.

"Can we try my father?" I ask through numb lips.

I have no desire to talk to him, but my mother doesn't have a phone. One more way he controls her.

"Of course."

I hold my breath as the phone rings and almost burst into tears as it picks up.

"Dad?"

"Amanda? Where are you?"

"This is going to sound crazy," I say. "But I was taken by the Grivath. The Arcav saved us, but we're still on the ship. Please...tell me how Bree is?"

"Are you drunk?" His voice is hard, and I flinch.

"Of course not. I'll be home soon, but I need to know how she's doing. She's not answering her phone."

"You expect me to believe you've been abducted by aliens? Either you're on drugs or you've had a psychotic break. Which one is it?"

"Dad, please—"

"Enough. You can see how she is yourself when you show up at the hospital like an adult, without a ridiculous story."

He hangs up, and I stand, wanting nothing more than to smash the screen in frustration.

"Call again," Jaret orders.

"There's no point," I sigh, rubbing my temple, where a vicious headache has decided to live. "He'll never tell me now."

Jaret ignores me, glancing at Zarbi, who immediately

calls back.

As predicted, my father doesn't pick up.

Jaret simply continues to call, again and again, until my father finally answers.

"I told you—"

"Peter Ashbury," Jaret says, voice like winter. I wonder how he found out my father's full name. "You are speaking to the Arcav commander. You will give your daughter a full update of her sister's status, or I will send an Arcav to the hospital to do it for me. Which would you prefer?"

My father is silent, and I can practically hear him grinding his teeth.

"My daughter is in a coma," he says and hangs up.

I'm rocking, distantly wondering what that sound is before I realize it's me, keening as I fall apart.

The last time I saw Bree, she was smiling. Every breath was a chore, each movement exhausting, but she was still smiling even as she planned her funeral. She insisted I wear the same bright colors I wear every day.

"No black for you, Manda. I'll haunt you if you try."

Now she's in a coma.

I once asked Bree how she dealt with it. How she lived, knowing she wasn't going to get the time everyone else would get.

"Nothing in life is guaranteed," she told me. "You could walk out in front of a truck tomorrow and I'd outlive you," she teased.

I gave her a look, and she took my hand.

"Every moment is more precious when it's not guaranteed. Would I rather be healthy? Of course. But this disease makes me appreciate the time I have."

Strong arms lift me up, and I clutch onto Jaret's shirt, soaking it with my tears. One day, maybe I'll be embarrassed at how he watched me crumple. But for now, I need someone, anyone, to hold on to.

Jaret

I leave Amanda curled up and sobbing in her bed. There is nothing I can do or say to make this time easier for her unless I can ensure her return to Earth.

Varian is waiting for me when I get back to the ComScreen.

"I need to take the ship to Earth."

He looks as surprised as I've ever seen him.

"Why would you need to do that?" His tone warns me to be careful even as his face lights up as Harlow appears, planting herself in his lap.

"Oh, hey, Jaret. Make any babies cry lately?"

I ignore her until I see the expectant look on Varian's face.

"Hello, Your Majesty," I say, well aware the female hates any form of title.

"Oooh, burn," she says, although she's smiling.

Varian pulls her closer, tucking her head under his chin.

"Why do you believe you must go back to Earth? As I communicated earlier, I need you to return to Arcavia."

"There is a human female," I begin, ignoring Harlow's slow smile. "She must get back to say goodbye to her sister, who is dying."

Harlow's smile drops, and tears immediately fill her eyes. Varian tilts his head, gazing down at her with a horrified expression, which immediately turns into a glare as he raises his eyes to me.

"Wow, that's so sad." Harlow sniffs, her pale face turning red. I sigh impatiently. I have never seen so many females crying as I have in the past three days.

"Harlow," Varian says carefully, "is it the horror moans?"

She lets out a snorted laugh. "It's *hormones*, big guy. And no. Well, maybe a little. I just can't imagine what she's going through."

"Do I have permission to change our flight path, Your Majesty?"

Varian frowns as he removes his attention from his mate. "As I specified, I need you to return immediately. Your ship is required to travel to Fecax."

I reach out and turn off the ComScreen.

I resist the urge to answer the ComCall as Varian immediately attempts to reconnect. For the first time, I am furious with him.

Varian and I grew up together. I have no real friends, but our relationship is more than just king and commander. My loyalty has always been to him and by extension, the Arcav people.

Yet when I have asked for something important, he has denied me.

I stride out of the room and find Amanda where I left her, curled in bed. She opens her eyes, and the hope in them is like a knife to my gut.

"I am sorry."

She closes her eyes. "Leave."

I give her privacy, feeling useless for the first time in centuries.

She will be able to depart for Earth as soon as we land. Do not let one small human make you forget your goals.

I straighten my shoulders and strengthen my resolve. I did not even ask Varian why he needed to send this ship to

Fecax. Perhaps the Grivath are attempting to invade. Any mission that involves the Grivath is more important than transporting one human back to Earth.

I spend the rest of the day in the control center. I am well aware my dark mood is impacting my men, and when I tear down a general for poor work, which is, in reality, almost perfect, Roax gives me a steady look.

"I will go," I tell him, and he simply nods.

I find Amanda with the other humans. Her eyes are swollen, and her face is pale, but she is attempting to distract herself. Her low, throaty laugh hits me, but her eyes do not light up.

She nods as she sees me, but her gaze reminds me of my own. Cold, blank, lifeless.

I gesture for her to join me, and she gets up without a word to the other women, following me without protest.

I lead her back to her room, selfishly wanting to keep her sad smiles to myself.

"What is it?" she asks, but her voice is hollow. I want to shake her out of this depression, but I can almost understand it. If I had a sibling, I would do anything I could to stay close if they were ill.

She sits on the edge of her bed as she looks up at me, but it's as if she does not see me, her blank expression telling me her thoughts are elsewhere.

"I have arranged for another ship to take you back to Earth once we arrive in Arcavia. We must wait two days before we leave as I must attend a ceremony. Varian is having a weeding with Harlow."

Amusement dances across her face. "You mean a wedding?"

I shrug.

She narrows her eyes. "Why do you have to come with me to Earth? Why can't I just go as soon as we land?"

"These are my terms, little human. Now you will thank me," I say silkily.

"Thank you. I—"

"You will do something for me."

"Of course. What—"

"You will kiss me."

Her eyes widen as I step closer.

"Why?"

"Arcav do not do this, but your people have taught us this skill. I have been told this is a unique experience."

"Uh, okay."

My horns straighten at her acceptance. She must feel it too—this chemistry between us.

She moves closer, and my claws extend as she inserts herself into my space, her lithe body molding to mine.

She gives me a shy smile, but the look in her eyes is anything but shy as she reaches up one hand, stroking my shoulder.

"We're a little mismatched," she says. "You'll need to lean down."

I comply, bending until our lips are so close that I can feel her warm breath on mine.

I wait for her to do this kiss. I have recently seen mated Arcav completing this activity almost everywhere I look in Arcavia.

Amanda leans closer, touching her lips to mine, and then she moves her hand to the back of my neck, holding me for balance. She rubs her lips against mine, and I instantly harden, almost trembling as her sweet, floral scent surrounds me.

"Kissing is kinda a two-person sport," she mumbles

against my mouth, and I nod, reaching out and pulling her close as the intoxicating scent of her desire hits me like thunder.

She opens her mouth under my assault, and I take a moment to play, stroking her tongue with mine as she groans.

She pulls away, looking up at me with dazed eyes. "Was that your first kiss?"

I give one sharp nod.

"Typical Arcav overachiever," she says, voice throaty, and reaches for me again.

I pull back, setting her away.

"I must go," I say and stalk out of her room.

I avoid her eyes, which are likely wounded from my unexpected retreat. It is all making sense now. I stare at my mating bands, which seem to vibrate slightly, as if urging me to return to the female who may be...my mate.

When we land in Arcavia, I will ask for her blood to be run against mine to see if it is a match. But deep down, I am already certain it is. My actions since I met her have not been those of a madman. They are the actions of a male who is going through the early mating period.

I feel a jolt of triumph as I realize Amanda will not be staying on Earth. She will be returning to Arcavia with me after she has seen her sister.

I may not be able to mate with her, but I will keep her close enough to see her every day for the rest of my life.

CHAPTER SEVEN

Amanda

Well, that was weird.
  Jaret kissed the hell out of me, glowered at me like I was his enemy, and then basically ran out of here like his horns were on fire.

I shake it off. I know kissing is a human thing, so it's likely the guy wanted to see what the big deal was. Honestly, I'm so grateful for his help that I would've kissed him for a lot longer than that.

I snort. Who am I kidding? I wasn't thinking about my gratitude while his tongue was in my mouth or when his hot, hard body was pressed against mine and his hands stroked me like I was something precious.

I rinse my face, removing any trace of tears. I just need to get through the next few days, and then I'll be heading back to Bree. A sudden pang of sadness hits me, and I pause. Am I...upset I won't be near the ice-cold commander anymore?

He wasn't ice cold when he kissed you.

That's definitely true. He was burning hot. The man is a

conundrum. It's as if he keeps the burning, beating heart of himself hidden behind a wall of ice.

I make my way back to the humans, assuming I'm allowed to wander around the ship now that Jaret knows I'm not going to try to steal a ride back to Earth. I find Veronica curled up next to a window, staring dully at the vast blackness beyond.

"Veronica?"

She lifts her eyes to mine, and they're drenched. I check for anyone within hearing distance and then sit down beside her.

"Hey," I whisper. "We're going home."

Her eyes widen, but her face remains blank as if she's too scared to believe me. "That's what you said last time."

"I know, I'm sorry. But this time, Jaret has arranged for us to leave soon after we get back to Arcavia."

Her face lightens with every word, and her deep-brown eyes clear. "Are you serious?"

"As an invasion."

"I'll be back with my babies," she says, clutching my hand. "How long?"

"A couple of days, apparently. I wouldn't be surprised if they step on the gas, honestly."

She sighs. "As much as we both wish it were sooner, we must try to accept it and be grateful they will return us home. Thank you for telling me. I'm sorry for snapping."

"I get it, Veronica. I can't imagine how scared you feel being separated from your kids."

We spend the rest of the day hanging out. Now that I know I'm going home, I focus on memorizing each moment of this experience. Once my feet are firmly back on Earth, that's where I'll be staying, but I know that if—no, *when*—Bree wakes up, she'll want me to tell her everything.

Eventually, I get bored and make my way back to my room. I stop by Jaret's quarters and hesitate, fist hovering in midair as I almost pound on the door.

"Bad idea, Amanda," I mutter and turn to go, just as the door opens.

"Don't mind me," I say. "I was having a moment of temporary insanity."

Jaret eyes me. "You are mentally unwell?"

"No." I snort. "That was a joke."

He stares at me like he can't quite figure me out. *The feeling is mutual, buddy.*

"Would you like to come in?"

"Um, sure."

I step inside, inhaling his masculine scent like a junkie. How is it I have this kind of chemistry with a man who left me chained up in a cell with a dead body?

His eyes are still cold, but every now and again, I see hints of emotion. I want to chip away at his ice wall until it shatters into a million pieces.

I avoid the bed and instead head toward the small sitting area connected to his bedroom. He follows me in, watching as I slump down on the sofa. The furniture here is way cooler than anything we have on Earth. It's made of some kind of gel, which immediately cradles my body as if it can tell exactly where my aches and pains are located.

"Tell me about your sister," Jaret orders, and I resist the urge to teach him some manners.

He sits next to me on the couch, ignoring the armchairs on either side of us, and I push down a spark of pleasure at his choice.

"My favorite subject right now. Let's see. She was born seven minutes before me, which makes me the little sister." I give him a wry grin, and he raises a brow.

"Seven minutes? How is this possible?"

"Ummm, you guys don't have twins?"

"I have not heard this word before."

Time for a rundown on human biology.

"Sometimes, an egg splits in two after it's been fertilized. Then the twins will be identical. In our case, two eggs were released and fertilized and we're not identical. Bree's prettier than me. But then again, she has cystic fibrosis, so you win some, you lose some."

My voice is bitter, and I try to get back on the right track. Jaret's eyes are taking in my every movement, a slight frown on his face as he listens to me talk.

"Anyway, multiples aren't super common, but they still happen regularly on Earth. One of Bree's friends had triplets recently. You guys don't have this?"

"No. I have never heard of such a thing. So you and your sister were in the womb together?"

"That's right. Probably elbowing each other and jostling for space. Bree likes to say I kicked her out first so I could take some time for myself in there." I grin.

"This is why you are so close."

"I dunno. We know other twins who were super competitive growing up. I think it was a combination of her sickness and our parents' crappy ideas about parenting that made us bond the way we did."

"You do not miss your mother and father?"

I sink down deeper into the sofa and sigh. "It's complicated. My parents are very religious and ridiculously strict. My father is a cold, arrogant control freak. When I was a teenager, he'd threaten to send me away to boarding school if I displeased him. He knew what it would do to me to be away from Bree when she was sick. During college, I was desperate to get out of his house, but he refused to let me move out. He would do things like ban Bree's friends from visiting the hospital when she annoyed him or attempt to get between us when he felt we were spending too much time together."

I catch the frown on his face and bite my lip. "Sorry for unloading."

His gaze is on my mouth, and I remove my teeth as his eyes finally meet mine.

"What about your mother?"

I shrug. "My mom married the wrong man. She doesn't have the strength to go up against him—probably because he sucked any strength out of her over forty years of marriage."

"What do you do in your free time?"

I narrow my eyes. "Is this some kinda interview?" I tease. "Why don't you tell me about your parents?"

"They are deceased."

Oh shit. "I'm so sorry."

He nods, and a muscle thumps in his jaw. Obviously, he doesn't want to talk about it.

"Um, I go out with friends. I used to work before you guys landed and I was laid off." I shoot him a dark look, and the ghost of a smile crosses his lips. God, if this guy actually smiled, it would be blinding. It's probably for the best that he doesn't.

"What else?"

I sigh. "I hang out with Bree. I collect elements," I say suddenly, unsure why I'm sharing this with him. "I'd show you my collection, but it's in Bree's hospital room."

I feel like an idiot. When we're alone, it's sometimes easy to forget I'm talking to the Arcav commander.

"Never mind," I say. "You've probably seen much more impressive things in Arcavia."

"No," he says slowly, his gaze on my mouth. "I would like to see your...collection."

He lingers over the word like it's dirty, and I get the feeling my element collection isn't the only thing he'd like to see. Something about his intense gaze has my skin heating as I shift.

"Tell me something about yourself," I say. "Who are your friends?"

"I do not have friends."

He leans forward, stroking the edge of a claw along my neck, and I blow out a breath as he continues.

"There is only one thing about me you need to know. My one reason for existence is to remove all Grivath from this universe. Be aware, little one," he warns. "I will do anything to see this happen, no matter the consequences."

"Why?" I whisper, staring at him, frozen like a rabbit in a trap.

His voice lowers even further. "Because they killed my parents."

Jaret

Most people—whether human or Arcav, Fecax, or even Grivath—have a defining moment. These are the moments that change the trajectory of our lives. For better or for worse.

For some, it is a new career or the birth of a child.

For Korva, it was when he lost his mate. That moment changed the future for both the Arcav and human races.

For Varian, it was the moment his mate ran from him.

For me, it was the moment my mother was murdered.

My mother was light and laughter, sunshine and smiles. She brightened every room yet insisted on fighting with my father, protecting Arcavia from a Grivath invasion.

Just a few centuries ago, females and males fought side by side. While males still had a natural tendency to protect, they also knew Arcav females were clever, vicious fighters.

My mother was taken hostage and killed when Varian's father, Aeton, refused to let the Grivath enter Arcavian airspace.

The Grivath showed the royal family and their guards every second of her death.

I like to imagine it was quick. In my gut, I know it was not.

I do not blame Aeton. I would have made the same choice. You do not risk the life of millions for the life of one. But Aeton and my father were best friends. My father watched my mother die on a ComScreen, howling as guards held him back as he tried to kill Aeton, the Arcav king.

My father took his own life three days later.

My hatred for the Grivath has continued to grow over the years as they invade planet after planet, enslaving people and killing creatures across the galaxy.

How many children have had to grow up motherless because of the Grivath?

Perhaps, if I had not been raised by my mother's sadistic brother, I would have recovered from her death.

"You are alive for one reason and one reason only. Do not imagine that because you are close to the Arcav prince, you are in any way special. You will find the Grivath who killed your parents and make them suffer."

My uncle is cruel and vicious, but he is right.

CHAPTER EIGHT

Amanda

It's difficult to keep track of time on the ship. But we land in Arcavia the next day. I've never felt so useless, and all I want to do is jump on another ship and get back to Earth.

Jaret has been avoiding me ever since we talked about our families. It's as if he sees his admission of his plan to wipe out the Grivath as a weakness. I shiver as I remember the look in his eyes as he gave me his warning. And it *was* a warning. I would never want to be stupid enough to get between him and his quest for vengeance.

Arcavia reminds me of a cross between a fairy-tale forest and a futuristic city, which doesn't surprise me at all. Jaret directs me into a pod, and we head toward a huge palace that seems to be made almost entirely of glass. I don't think I'll ever get used to the feeling of zipping through the air, and my stomach lurches as we zigzag in and out of traffic.

The air is thinner here, and I occasionally feel like I'm gulping to get enough oxygen. According to the Arcav, this is normal and I'll adjust within a few days.

Jaret shoots me strange looks occasionally, but all I can do is gasp as I stare out the window.

No wonder he's so disparaging of Earth.

I wish I had a journal to make notes for Bree. I want to write about everything I see, but instead I try to soak it in, taking pictures with my mind so I can tell her every last detail.

I've decided she's *not* dying. The only way I can get through the next few days is to pretend she's sitting up in her hospital bed, waiting for me to come and regale her with stories about space travel.

So that's what I'm planning to do.

Veronica decided to go hang out with the other human women when Jaret declared I would be going with him. Truthfully, I was more than willing to spend time with the ice man. I've got it bad.

We land and walk into the palace, entering a huge room. It reminds me of a cathedral, with stained glass windows and marble floors, but it's about as busy as Grand Central Station at rush hour.

Heads turn as Arcav greet Jaret, who raises his hand but doesn't deign to stop. We're heading toward a more heavily guarded part of the palace, and I'm out of breath trying to keep up with Jaret's long strides.

"Where are we going?"

"I must talk to Varian." Jaret glances at me and then continues to stalk through the hall.

"Is there somewhere I can wait?" I ask, and he frowns.

"Why?"

"I can't come with you to meet the Arcav king," I hiss. "I'm wearing jeans!"

His lip curls, and for a moment, my heart stops as he almost smiles.

"The queen often wears the same strange blue leg coverings."

"Wow, really?"

Huh. Royalty—they're just like us. I do remember the queen used to be a cop, and according to the media on Earth, she really gave the Arcav king a run for his money when she bolted.

"Jaret, can't I just meet them later? Please?"

He shakes his head, and I stop dead, frustrated. He turns, brow lowering, and sunlight from a large window bathes his face in a soft glow. He looks like an angel. A tormented, warrior angel with horns instead of wings.

"What is it you need from me, Amanda? Do you wish for me to tell you how beautiful you are so that you will feel comfortable in my king's presence?"

He's not an angel. He's a demon.

"Forget it," I snap. "Let's go."

He leads me silently down one more hall and nods to the guards outside a huge door. They open it, and we enter a large, impeccably decorated sitting room. It's quiet, with light entering from the large windows and hitting various crystals around the room.

A woman is lying on a sofa reading a book. She looks up as we enter, locking eyes with Jaret.

"Oh," she says, waving a hand with a smirk. "It's you."

He frowns at her. "Your Majesty."

She snorts and drops her long legs to the ground as my mouth drops open. *This* is the Arcav queen?

She's wearing leggings and an oversized sweater. Her hair is disheveled in a way that tells me she was either recently napping or recently getting lucky. From the content look on her face, I'm guessing the latter. She meets my eyes and smiles, and I realize I'm staring.

"Not what you were expecting?"

I grin back. Something about her encourages me to relax.

"I kind of imagined you waltzing around in a gown with a crown on your head. Maybe even clutching a scepter."

She snorts again, but her smile widens.

"Varian would love that. I'm Harlow," she says. "And forget about any titles—Jaret just does it to annoy me."

How is this woman so beautiful but also so down-to-earth? I'm officially starstruck.

"I'm Amanda."

Her face softens in sympathy. "You're the one with the sister..."

I flinch, and tears fill her eyes.

The Arcav king chooses that moment to enter, huge and intimidating. He takes one look at Harlow's face, and his eyes widen in something that might be panic.

"What is wrong?"

Varian pulls her close, staring down at her, and my heart clenches. He looks at her with a furious protectiveness, like he'll do anything to keep her safe and happy—and God help anyone who attempts to harm her. Every woman deserves to be looked at that way.

Harlow clears her throat. "I'm fine."

She smiles up at him, and their love is so blinding that I look away, meeting Jaret's gaze. I don't like the knowing look on his face, so I stare out the window at the wild garden.

"This is Amanda," Harlow says, and I turn back as Varian nods to me and then immediately returns his eyes to his mate. I almost laugh, finally relaxing. I could've walked in here naked, clucking like a chicken, and neither of them would've noticed, their eyes only for each other.

It's beautiful to see, and I smile, burying my envy.

I'd never admit it to anyone, but in the most secret part of my soul, locked away where no one can see it, I keep a secret wish. A wish for an epic love. One for the ages. The kind of love that breaks you to pieces but then puts you back together again, better than you were before.

Even witnessing my father's cold mistreatment of my mother couldn't kill this dream. I just longed harder for a man who burned with a fierce love of life. A man who would be an open book—quick to laugh and eager to experience everything life has to offer.

I meet Jaret's cold, blank gaze again as Harlow finally drags her eyes from Varian and clears her throat.

She smiles at me. "We're actually having a small ceremony tomorrow, similar to a human wedding. At least it was supposed to be small," she says, sliding a glance at Varian. "I know you're probably not in a partying mood, but I'd love for you to come along."

I smile. Well, if I'm going to be stuck here while I wait anyway... "My sister would expect nothing less. I'd be honored to come."

Jaret

I find Amanda a room close to the royal quarters, at Harlow's insistence. I have my own quarters here but often prefer to stay in my childhood home on the outskirts of the city.

I visit, wandering the large estate. Sometimes, I imagine I can hear my parents' voices. For years, I would occasionally wake up and forget they were gone, rushing to the kitchen, where I would find my uncle instead, looming like a dark cloud.

Every morning, we would have the same conversation.

"What is your goal in life, son?" I grit my teeth. I hate when he calls me son, and he knows it. He seems intent on stepping into my father's place in public so he can be seen as the generous, loving brother raising his nephew as his own.

In reality, the only time he deigns to pay me any attention in private is when he is beating me or planning my revenge.

"Avenge my parents."

"And how will you avenge them?"

I blink up at him. I am only ten years old and do not yet know how. All I know is the Grivath took my parents from me, and they will pay.

"I will not stop until every last Grivath is dead."

"Good. Very good."

I turn from the kitchen. Maybe I should sell this estate. Or perhaps even have it destroyed. My uncle insisted on moving in here with his mate, a young Arcav female who both loved and loathed him in equal measure. Those years were some of the worst of my life.

And yet I imagine I can still smell my mother's scent in her sitting room. I can occasionally hear my father's low, gruff laugh on a windy day.

I do not know why I have come here. I do not have time. I wander the grounds, stopping to brush a finger over one of the flowers my mother said reminded her of a rainbow. My thoughts immediately return to Amanda. She would love this place.

I have never taken a woman back here. Not even Brexa. But I find myself wanting to see Amanda's face light up, her eyes widening the way they did when we traveled in the pod.

The thought of Amanda in my mother's gardens, her avid gaze drinking up each new sight, makes me want things I can never have.

I lock the front door with my palm print and make my way back to Varian's quarters.

"Harlow needs to sleep," he says, his gaze shifting toward their bedroom. "She is much more tired these days."

I nod. "I must return to Earth directly after your ceremony."

His brow arches. "You will return with the human?"

"I believe she may be my mate."

"Ah. Is she aware of this?"

I shake my head, and he waits for me to elaborate, finally changing the subject after a moment of silence.

"Harlow insisted I need a 'best man' for this ceremony. You are the best man I know, so you must fill this position."

"What does a best man do?"

Varian shrugs. "Stand next to me and be better than the other men?"

We both frown as we contemplate these strange human customs.

I nod. "Excuse me. I must go to Brexa."

"Will you tell her you have mated?"

"I may have a mate, but we have not mated."

Varian's grin is savage. "Ahh, old friend. It is only a matter of time."

I grit my teeth as I leave. I preferred Varian when he was crazed, determined, and lonely. Like me. Now he is quicker to laugh, more willing to relax, and obsessed with his mate's happiness.

I am in a dark mood when I reach Brexa's home. She pulls open her door with a laugh and rushes to me, throwing herself into my arms.

I attempt to ignore the sense of wrongness that hits me with her scent as I firm my shoulders. Mating may not be a choice, but acting on that mating is.

I follow Brexa inside.

"I need information."

She pouts prettily. Everything Brexa does is pretty. She is as beautiful as an ice sculpture and just as cold. We are well suited, she and I.

"But you just got back! Can we not spend some time together?"

"I must prepare for Varian's celebration and then will need to return to Earth."

Brexa smiles. "At least I will see you at the celebration."

I grit my teeth but nod. Brexa is Varian's cousin. She grew up spoiled and pampered and enjoys the fact I do not wish to be with her.

"Tell me what you have heard."

She sighs. "Must you always be this way, Jaret? I have missed you."

"You know our arrangement. If you did not blackmail me with information, I would not be seen with you in public. Would not allow you to tell your friends I am in your bed."

Her eyes flash, and she turns, stalking to her room. I sigh. I know better than to remind Brexa of my dislike for her. Now she will be even more difficult.

I debate leaving, but if I am to put up with this female, I must know of the Grivath's movements.

"Brexa. Do not make me come in there."

I hear a muttered curse and sigh again. Her moods are turbulent, but she enjoys resorting to threats and emotional blackmail over the slightest insult. She walks back out, a frown on her face. Her eyes are shining, her lips bright, and she looks like a perfect doll. I have a sudden image of Amanda's ravaged face as she learned of her sister's health.

"What. Do. You. Know." I am losing patience, and Brexa pales, biting her lip.

"You do not need to be so rude to me," she says.

I quash the urge to destroy everything in this room. My moods have never been stable, the rage quick to come and slow to leave. But I have never had a problem transforming that rage into cold action. Now I am one moment away from leveling this house.

I come here for one reason and one reason only. Brexa's former maid lives on Traslann. The Trasla are allied with the Grivath, and the maid has found work close to the Trasla's leader and president.

Chenda takes a risk with her surveillance, guaranteed a long, painful death if she is caught. And yet she is more loyal than Brexa, who will not contact her for information unless I come to her.

Brexa sighs, the frown disappearing from her face as if it were never there.

"I spoke to Chenda yesterday," she says. "She said the Grivath are preparing for something huge. She's not yet sure what it is, but she said the Trasla are reconsidering their alliance with the Grivath, as they are worried about the repercussions of being associated with them."

My heart quickens. This. *This* is why I put up with Brexa. With this information, we can potentially try to sway the Trasla to our side. If they were to ally with us instead, we would have intelligence on the Grivath like we have never had before.

Brexa reaches for me, and I soften. She smiles up at me, obviously assuming her attitude has been forgiven.

"I would like to try something," she says.

"Yes?"

"I would like to try this kissing the humans do."

I stiffen. "You hate the humans."

"I do not hate them." She sniffs. "I just do not want them in Arcavia. Besides, I do not need to like them in order to want to know why I am now suddenly seeing Arcav engage in this activity."

Brexa has the look in her eyes that tells me if I do not give her this one thing, she will make sure I am busy escorting her to events throughout Arcavia. She enjoys the notoriety and prestige of being associated with me, purely because I have the king's ear.

I shrug, lean down, and take her lips, immediately regretting it. Her lips are slack beneath mine. She tastes wrong, her body not conforming to mine, her scent too musky and headache-inducing.

I pull away, barely restraining myself from wiping my lips.

She smiles. "That was nice."

A first kiss should not be nice. If there is one thing I have learned from my kiss with Amanda, it is that a first kiss should be the opposite of nice.

"We will never do that again," I say, and her face hardens.

I leave before she can reply, finding Brin in the medi-center.

"I need your help," I say, and he raises an eyebrow as he looks up from his notes. Brin and I were friends as children, his mother best friends with mine. She attempted to reach out a few times after my parents' deaths, but I couldn't look at her without seeing my mother's face.

"What is it?" His tone is cool.

"I need some blood processed. I have met a human female who I believe may be my mate."

A slow smile spreads over his face, and I have an urge to hit him.

"This will be interesting," he says.

I hold out my finger, and he takes a drop of blood. Putting it on a slide, he then holds it under a scanner.

"Name?"

"Amanda Ashbury."

He presses a few buttons, and I close my eyes as the screen flashes green. I do not know what to feel.

"Congratulations."

I snarl, and he gives me that knowing smile again.

"Oh. You are still with Brexa. Interesting."

I ignore him. Brin, too, believes the gossip, assuming I am with Brexa. And he may think he understands why I am so often seen with her, but he has no idea.

"I need one more thing."

He waits patiently, and I am certain he will soon be starting a betting pool with his fellow healers based on my mating.

"I need you to access some medical records here. My mate's sister is dying. I believe I may have seen a similar disease to this a few centuries ago."

"What is it you are hoping for?"

I rub one of my horns. "I do not know. If there is a way for her to be healed in Arcavia, is it possible to bring her back?"

"It would depend on her condition. If she is close to death, she would need to be put into stasis. Even that process can occasionally be too much for a body to take. I will examine her records and let you know."

I nod and leave, restraining the urge to wipe the smirk

off Brin's face. By the time I reach Amanda's door, my mood is black, and I hesitate. I do not know what I am doing here, but I lift my hand and knock.

No answer.

I knock again, waiting for her to come to the door, and then sigh. I should not be surprised Amanda has decided to leave, likely to meet new people. She has the type of personality that attracts friends, and I often saw her chatting with both Arcav and humans on the ship.

"Oh, hi, Jaret."

I turn as Amanda walks toward me, waving goodbye to another human female, who gives me a knowing look. Amanda looks so fresh and innocent and nothing like Brexa, and I suddenly growl, frustration coursing through me as I pull her into my arms and take her mouth.

CHAPTER NINE

Amanda

How did Jaret learn to kiss like this? Is it instinctive, or is he just an insanely fast learner? That's all I think before my mind blanks, and it's like I'm scuba diving again or flying through space, completely untethered. I soak up every moment of his touch. His hands are firm on me, and a growl sounds low in his chest as he backs me against the wall. His hands push mine above my head, and he leans closer, covering me with his huge body.

"Ahem."

I jolt and push at Jaret's chest, although he seems content to simply ignore the interruption. He nips my lip, hard, and I pinch him in retaliation.

"Well, this is interesting."

Jaret pulls away, not deigning to look at Harlow, who is grinning as she taps one foot. Methi stands next to her, a similar shit-eating grin on his own face. I met him and a few of the other guards a couple of hours ago, and they couldn't have been more welcoming.

"Uh, Harlow." It feels weird to not call her by a title, but the last time I tried, she threatened to tit-punch me. "What can I do for you?"

She scans Jaret and opens her mouth.

"Too easy," she mutters, turning her attention back to me. "I was just thinking about the ceremony tomorrow. I'm guessing you don't have anything to wear, so I wanted to see if you'd like to come get ready with us? My closet puts Macy's to shame."

Jaret mutters under his breath and moves away, and something inside me mourns as his eyes dim and his face once again becomes cool and controlled.

One day, I'm going to make you completely lose that control. And it's going to be glorious.

I turn to Harlow. "That would be amazing. But are you sure I won't be crashing your party?"

She snorts and waves her hand. "Nah. We're all family here. The more the merrier. I'll leave you two to get back to whatever you were doing," she says with a sly smile, and Methi winks at me.

I eye Jaret as they leave. His face tells me he couldn't care less about people seeing us making out, and I know his discomfort is simply from others seeing him display something other than boredom or disinterest.

I'm beginning to notice the smallest changes on his face, and it scares me how much attention I pay to his moods. But I can tell something's bothering him.

"What's up?"

He frowns, and I sigh. Why does he have to look so rumpled and adorable yet completely unapproachable at the same time?

"You look upset."

His face hardens. "I am fine."

Okay, then.

I expect him to leave, but he leads me to a small sitting room in the guest quarters. He gestures toward a sofa and sits next to me. Close but somehow too far away.

"I wish to learn more about you."

I shrug. "There's not much to say, really. I'm pretty boring."

"Tell me about your collection."

This man drives me crazy. Speaking with him is like being interrogated. He constantly insists on asking me questions but refuses to talk even a little about himself. On the ship, he questioned me about everything from my high school years to what I like to eat for breakfast. And yet he won't open up at all.

"How about we make it a game?"

"A game?" Jaret looks confused at the thought, and my heart clenches. When was the last time this guy just had fun?

"Yeah." I smile as that slight crease appears between his eyes again. "We take turns asking each other questions. If you don't want to answer a question, then you lose. And then you have to do something for the other person."

His eyes scan me, and I shiver, blowing out a breath as he takes a moment to think it over.

"It's just a game, Jaret. I'm not asking for your firstborn."

He continues to study my face and then finally nods. I grin, feeling ridiculously pleased he'll play with me.

"I will go first," he says.

"I'd expect nothing less."

"Why did you choose your hobby?"

I blank. "Huh?"

"Your elements. You could have collected anything, but you chose these. Why?"

Wow, the guy really digs in deep.

"When I was small, I asked our priest how elements could exist if the universe was created by God. Unlike my father, who considered those types of questions to be blasphemy, the priest was more than willing to answer my questions."

Jaret shifts closer, and I look away, vulnerability hitting me hard.

I clear my throat. "He told me to think of them as God's bricks. He said maybe they were the tools God used to create the universe."

I grin at him, but for some reason, I feel perilously close to crying.

"Anyway, from that moment, I had a mission. I was obsessed with collecting as many God bricks as I could, certain if I could find them all, I'd have the power to fix my sister."

I wipe away a tear and laugh. "Don't judge me too harshly. I was only nine."

"You were goal-oriented," Jaret says, and I laugh.

"That's one way to put it. Once I was old enough to understand I couldn't make Bree better, no matter how many elements I collected, I still continued to collect them anyway. When I was stressed, I'd focus on the periodic table or take out my collection and look at the elements I'd managed to find over the years."

I blow out a breath. *I'll see you soon, Bree.*

"How many elements are there on Arcavia?" I ask.

Jaret reaches out and runs his finger along my collarbone. My stomach muscles clench, and then I curse as I realize I just wasted my question. I move further out of reach, glaring at him as his eyes lighten in amusement.

"Two hundred and thirty-four," he says softly. "Which element is your favorite?"

I smile. "Honestly, some of my favorites are the ones that are too difficult for me to get my hands on. I like elements that react. No surprise there. Fluorine is the most reactive. If you just blow a stream of the gas at an object, it'll usually burst into flame. Even things that aren't flammable."

I've never known a man who paid such close attention to me when I speak, but it feels like Jaret is filing away my words.

"Why are you coming back with me to Earth?" I ask.

He pushes some hair off my face and tucks it behind my ear.

"I do not seem to be able to allow you to go without me."

I open my mouth, but he simply shakes his head, shutting down that line of conversation. "Tell me something about you that nobody else knows."

I think furiously for a moment, but I've got nothing.

"Sorry, I tell Bree everything." I smile. "We're a little codependent that way."

"Something that only she knows, then."

I take a breath. "Don't laugh." I snort. "Who am I talking to? Okay. I started doing this thing when I was a kid, where I would choose an element to represent everyone I knew."

He nods, as if that's the most normal thing in the world, and I relax a little. "So, like, Bree is carbon. My high school math teacher was arsenic. My best friend was zinc."

"Keep going."

"My father is cadmium. It used to be found in batteries, but now it's mostly replaced by options that are more powerful, lighter, and less toxic." I smirk. "Cadmium accumulates in the body and the environment—just like mercury or lead—causing long-term damage to life wherever it's found."

Jaret seems to be storing away this information. "And your mother?"

I sigh. "Argon. It comes from the Greek word for 'inactive.' It's a cheap, completely inert gas that breaks down and is entirely uninteresting in combination with other chemicals. You can buy it at most stores. The one decent use for it? It can prevent wine from oxidizing, which if you knew my mother, would be about as ironic as it gets."

This conversation is making me long for a glass of wine myself.

"My turn," I say, but Jaret simply shakes his head, running the back of one claw down my throat as I shiver.

"What do you want, Amanda?"

I raise a brow. "What anyone wants. To be happy."

It doesn't look like that answer has satisfied him.

"I will never be able to make you happy," he says suddenly, although he moves even closer.

"Why?" I whisper as his gaze locks onto my lips.

He ignores me, leans down, and kisses me. Instantly, my body feels languid, and he cups my head as it rolls back against the sofa. Then I'm moving, and my eyes fly open as he positions me on top of him, straddling him almost indecently in my colorful skirt.

"I like this," he says, stroking the thin material. "It is vivid and vibrant, just like you."

I flush with pleasure, and he uses that moment to take my mouth again. It's as if he's sucked all the oxygen out of the room and his mouth is the only place to find it.

His kiss is possessive, and I groan as his hands wander along my back and settle on my butt, where they cup me, nestling me close to him. I grind against his hardness, and he pulls back, looking down at me with heavy-lidded eyes.

Jaret's hand slips under my skirt and find its way to my heat, where he strokes, his mouth curling in satisfaction. I spot the hint of a fang and reach out, using one finger to lift his upper lip. I never see these, I realize, because this man keeps himself ruthlessly in control.

Jaret continues to stroke, and I let my hand fall as I gasp. God, he's good at that. I feel a pang of jealousy, hating all the women he's practiced on over the centuries, and then I'm writhing against him, no longer able to think.

He leans forward and pushes my bra down with his other hand. His mouth finds my nipple, and my breath stops as I come so hard I can't make a single sound.

CHAPTER TEN

Amanda

"Champagne?"

I reach for the glass, grinning at Eve. Apparently, she's one of Harlow's guards. All I know is she's hilarious and Harlow had to threaten her with everything under the sun to make her wear a dress. Harlow finally told her if she didn't stop acting like a little bitch, she'd change the seating plan for dinner and put her next to Korva.

I've only seen the man once, and he merely nodded before proceeding to ignore everyone and everything around him. But for some reason, Eve paled and then flushed, gritting her teeth and holding out her hand for the dress.

"You win this time, Maleficent. But my revenge will be sweet."

Harlow merely smirked and wandered off, still wearing her pajamas.

I take a sip of my champagne, doing my best to dampen the thread of guilt that's sewn through my every moment away from Bree. I *know* she'd want me to enjoy myself, but if I could have one wish, it'd be that she was here with me, gulping champagne and likely becoming firm friends with Eve.

I do everything I can not to think about the Arcav who left me heavy-eyed and breathless on the sofa yesterday, striding out the door with fury on his face and a bulge in his pants.

I've never met a man who runs so hot and cold in my life.

Meghan appears with a long silver gown in her hand.

"Okay, so I know you said you'd take a look at the dresses later, but I saw this and immediately thought of you. You'd look banging."

I raise an eyebrow. "It's very...shiny."

"I know, I know, but everyone will be going full glam. Now's your chance to relive those prom days, you know? Only, without the weird eighties haircut." She bursts out laughing as my mouth drops open.

"I'm a millennial!"

"I'm just playing. But really, put it on. Don't make me get Harlow involved."

The woman in question is currently sitting in front of her vanity as her maid, Minerva, works on her makeup and hair. She quirks an eyebrow at her name and turns, eyeing both of us.

"Put on the dress," she says and smirks. "My day, my way, remember?"

"Jeez. Okay, I'll try it on, but if my tits are falling out, I reserve the right to try something else."

She simply nods and turns back to the mirror.

"For a woman who could otherwise order everyone to

kiss her butt and yet refuses to, Harlow's really enjoying being a bridezilla," Meghan mutters.

"Heard that."

Meghan winks at me, and I get up, shucking out of my clothes and pulling the dress over my head. It fits like a glove, hugging all the right places, and Meghan does a little victory dance as I make my way over to the mirror.

My tits aren't falling out, but they're definitely not hiding away either. In spite of the sparkles and the fit, the dress still remains classy.

I turn. "What do you guys think?"

Harlow claps her hands, once again jostling Minerva, who simply steps back, giving me a smile while Harlow spins.

"You look amazing. Seriously."

"Okay, but it's not too much, is it? I don't want to be that woman who shows up dressed like she's trying to look better than the bride."

Harlow bursts out laughing. "Honestly, Varian has gone full diva with my dress. You've got nothing to worry about."

"Wait. He chose your dress?"

She waves a hand and sits back down. "I let him give some directions to the designers, but he hasn't seen the finished product. Neither have I, though, so..." She gives a shrug.

Wow.

Meghan hands Harlow a glass of champagne, and she sighs, takes a small sip, and then hands it back.

"If I weren't knocked up, I'd slam that so hard..."

My mouth drops open, and she winks at me as the room goes completely silent before shrieks sound from every direction.

I wince as about twenty women emit sounds that could

crack glass, descending on Harlow like she just announced she's got winning lottery numbers hidden in her purse.

"Well, holy shit," Eve says. "That explains the attitude."

Harlow narrows her eyes at her and then grins. "The hormones have been a bitch. Varian's not complaining though."

Cackles and catcalls sound, and I smile, soaking in this moment. I can't wait to give Bree a play-by-play of every second on Arcavia.

An older woman steps forward, giving Harlow a hug, and without warning, both of them burst into tears.

Harlow laughs, wiping her face. Poor Minerva simply sighs, collecting bottles and tubes she previously pushed away.

Harlow smiles at the older woman. "Can you believe it, Jen?"

"I hate to say I told you so..."

The women crack up, and then Meghan claps her hands.

"An hour until showtime, ladies. We still need to get Harlow in her dress."

"And where's *your* dress, honey?" Jen asks.

Meghan blushes. "I haven't chosen one yet."

Jen smiles and turns to the room. "Meghan never went to prom. So this is her first time wearing a formal gown."

The room erupts in high-pitched, feminine excitement.

"Aaaaw, so cute!"

"You should definitely wear pink!"

"With her skin tone? A jewel-color would be better."

"Anything but white."

Meghan turns a deep red, and Harlow grabs her hand.

"I put a little something aside for you earlier. If it's not your style, wear something else, but I thought you might like it."

Harlow winks at Minerva, who pulls a dress out of the closet, and everyone collectively inhales.

It's stunning.

"Wow...I can't wear that."

"Of course you can. Try it on, and if you don't like it, you can switch."

Meghan moves behind the changing screen, and light conversation breaks out. Finally, she steps out, and every woman in the room grins.

Jen tears up again. "Honey, you look gorgeous."

The dress is midnight blue, flecked with silver gems, which look like stars set against a night sky. It highlights her tiny waist and flares out, looking both sexy and somehow still age appropriate.

Meghan blushes, eyes uncertain, and for the first time, she looks her age. She's usually so mature and self-confident that my mouth dropped open when she announced she was turning seventeen in a few days.

Harlow grins. "Take a look in the mirror, Meghan."

Meghan obeys, stepping forward and gazing into the floor-length mirror.

"Wow," she says. "I'd do me."

Everyone cracks up, and Minerva finally taps Harlow on the shoulder, gesturing for her to hold still.

"Right," Harlow says. "Let's get this show on the road."

CHAPTER ELEVEN

Amanda

Harlow looks like a dream. The cut of her gown highlights her delicate neck and toned shoulders. The fabric sparkles with diamonds, and she holds her head high, grinning as her brother, Josh, walks her down the aisle to where her mate waits. The look on Varian's face brings tears to my eyes, and I wipe them away, meeting Jaret's gaze as he stands near the couple.

I return my attention to where Varian is gazing at Harlow as if she alone holds the key to the universe. She winks at him, his brow lowers, and he holds out his hand for hers, as if desperate to touch her.

Sighs sound as she finally reaches him, her crown sending rainbows dancing around the room.

"Check it out," she told us when Minerva appeared with it sparkling in her hands. "This thing is solid diamond." She passed it around the room for us all to try on, and I grin as I remember the look of despair on poor Minerva's face when a woman named Chloe almost refused to give it back.

Varian wastes no time, immediately leaning forward and kissing his mate, to the amusement of all the humans.

"It's not time for that yet, big guy," Harlow says, and he merely smiles, gazing into her eyes as if he can't quite believe his luck.

The ceremony is brief, their vows sweet. Harlow promises to "protect him from Tom" and "never again arrange for him to be kidnapped." Varian promises to "make sure she has chocolate close by at all times," "to tolerate Tom"– whoever *that* is– and "to always give her so much sex."

Snorts break out at that one, and Harlow turns red even as she laughs at Varian's smug grin.

Dinner is delicious, but I barely eat, too busy enjoying myself. Jen stands to give a speech, and the room goes silent.

"Harlow, I know how much your mom would've wanted to be here, and I truly believe she watched you walk down that aisle today. I've never seen two people who were as right for each other as you and Varian, and I wish you a long and happy marriage and mating."

To my surprise, Jaret stands next. His cool, dry tone has the whole room in hysterics as he describes Varian's confusion and disbelief that Harlow wasn't falling to her knees in gratitude at the chance to be his mate. Harlow howls with laughter as Jaret describes how Varian asked him to check her family history for mental defects—the only reason she would be running from him, of course.

Jaret retakes his seat as the room erupts in applause and cheering, and Harlow grins at me before nuzzling closer to Varian.

"That was great," I whisper and feel him tense next to me.

"What is wrong with your wrists?"

I frown as I examine them, realizing I've been scratching them again. I've left long red marks, which stand out, stark against my fair skin.

"I'm not sure. Must be a reaction to something here."

Jaret barely breathes beside me and then suddenly gets to his feet, stalking away from the table. Thankfully, people have gotten up, beginning to dance, and barely anyone notices he apparently doesn't want to be near me right now.

I grit my teeth and ignore the hurt. He's not my boyfriend. After I get back to Earth, I'll never see him again.

I dance with Harlow's friend Blake, who tells me he was her partner on Earth. He's got moves, and I'm howling with laughter by the time he finishes twirling me around the dance floor. Next, Methi takes my hand. He mutters something about human music and continuously glowers at Meghan, who looks resplendent as she dances with a human guy. She's carefully ignoring Methi, but her heart is in her eyes whenever she glances over at us until I finally urge him to go dance with her.

Eve is currently taking shots with a guy named Nathan, a seriously sexy man with a Southern accent. Her dress hugs her curves, and I don't know where Eve was hiding that body, but the girl is a knockout. Unfortunately, she looks about as comfortable in her long black gown as a cat taking a bath and scowls anytime anyone gives her a compliment.

"Hey, Small! Looking good!"

"Shut it, Josh, before I make you eat my fist."

I turn at a hand on my elbow and meet Jaret's eyes.

"Will you dance with me?"

I sigh. "Jaret—"

He simply takes my hand and leads me further into the center of the dance floor.

"You look stunning," he says, and I relax into him.

"I don't understand you."

"I know."

"You're so hot and cold."

"I know."

"Stop saying that!" I push away, suddenly furious, and he pulls me back to him.

"I wish I could be what you need."

"You could be," I hiss, "but this conversation is pointless. We're leaving tomorrow."

He frowns down at me but wisely changes the subject.

"Tell me...which one of your elements is she?" He nods toward Eve, who is grinning at Blake. The guy has just commandeered a bottle of whiskey from the bar and is currently pouring another round.

"Eve?" I think for a moment. "Zirconium. Tough, strong, and abrasive. But when it's a crystal, zirconium is cubic zirconia—a glittery, sparkly jewel."

Jaret nods toward Blake. That's tricky, since I've only talked to him for a couple of minutes. But something tells me he's deeper than he appears. He seems like he's missing something, or someone. His smile always comes a half second too late, his laugh often hollow.

"He's neodymium. Its best-known use is in neodymium magnets—the strongest available. So strong that they're dangerous to be around. You never want to get in between two of these magnets. If you have more than one, they'll literally jump toward each other, even if your finger or hand is in the way."

I grin, getting into the game, and make eye contact with Meghan, who is now dancing with Methi.

"Meghan is niobium. It makes the most beautiful colored jewelry, which reminds me of a mermaid. All pinks and blues, greens and purples," I tell him when he frowns.

Of course he doesn't know what a mermaid is. "Niobium is also corrosion resistant and about as hard as titanium."

Jaret nods, and I laugh.

"You don't know what any of these things are."

"I spent some time on Earth when Varian was looking for Harlow. Some of these elements sound the same as a few of those found on Arcavia." He leans closer and murmurs in my ear, "Besides, I enjoy the passion in your eyes and your explanation for each person."

I feel my cheeks heat and lower my eyes. This man makes me feel like a teenager.

"Continue," he says, and I shrug.

"Okay. Methi. Hmmm. Tin. Nontoxic, shiny, easy to form into different shapes. It was once used to make tin soldiers, although they were also made out of lead for a while, which was a bad time."

I eye Methi as he stares down at Meghan. "Tin is an inexpensive, inoffensive element. It's...useful. But in cold temperatures, it slowly transforms. There's no chemical change that happens, no oxidization or rusting. But...it changes. From a shiny silvery metal into a dark-gray powder."

I lock eyes with Korva, who glances away disinterestedly. His gaze finds Eve, who is now dancing in a group, head thrown back as she laughs.

Jaret follows my gaze and raises his eyebrow. I grin. I've already thought about this.

"Korva is neon. The least reactive of the elements. It glows bright and vivid yet completely refuses to react with any other elements."

I'm feeling pretty pleased with my party trick, when I lock eyes with an Arcav female. She's gorgeous—as all Arcav are. But her beauty has thorns. Her face is serene, yet her eyes hold the kind of animosity I've never seen directed at me before. At least not by a stranger.

She reaches us, and Jaret frowns as I stop dancing, turning to her. I keep my attention firmly on him as he looks at her and watch closely as annoyance, anger, and finally acceptance flash across his face.

These two have history.

"Jaret," she purrs, and I instantly hate her. "I would like to talk to you."

He shakes his head dismissively and turns back to me.

She simply lifts a brow, not sparing me a glance.

"It is important." She says it with complete confidence, and he tilts his head, turning back to her.

"It better be." Jaret releases me, and the places where his warm hands were touching me instantly feel cold. "I am sorry," he says through clenched teeth, and then he turns, following her without a backward glance.

I'm left standing on the dance floor alone, and I slink off to the bar, where Eve is panting from dancing as she hands me a shot.

"Don't worry," she says. "There's always tequila."

"Yes, there is."

I spend an hour hanging out with Eve, who avoids any mention of Jaret, obviously deducing the subject is not my favorite right now. Finally, I decide to look for him. Surely a simple conversation wouldn't take an hour in the middle of a wedding reception, right?

Half an hour later, I've looked everywhere, including in his quarters, after one of the guards recognized me and allowed me to check. I feel like a stalker, and I'm done wandering after him like a lost puppy.

I make my way back down to the reception and poke my head in the huge room, taking in the soft lights; wide, open windows; and flowers at every turn. Varian is sitting down, Harlow in his lap, and they're entirely wrapped up in each other, grinning as he strokes her flat stomach.

Meghan is gazing up into Methi's eyes. He looks tormented as she leans closer, pulling him toward her for a kiss. He jerks away, and she shakes her head at him sadly and then turns, walking away. Even from here I can see the tears glinting in her eyes.

Everyone else is either dancing or deep in conversation and unlikely to notice I'm gone.

I've borrowed a night in this world, but I'm an interloper. It's a good thing I realized this before I got any ideas about returning. My sister needs me, and tomorrow I'll be going back to Earth, where I should never have left.

Jaret

Amanda is silent the next day as we wait to board the ship that will take us back to Earth. She has not mentioned my disappearance last night, but the disinterested look in her eyes when she glances at me has my jaw aching from clenching my teeth.

Her eyes have tears in them when she hugs Harlow and her friends goodbye.

"Thank you for being so warm and welcoming. I had the most amazing time."

"I'm so glad. Good luck, and I'm sending your sister all the positive vibes in the universe," Harlow says, and Amanda's smile trembles for a moment before she firms it.

We wave goodbye, and I meet Varian's eyes. Our conversation last night after I talked to Brexa lingers between us.

Whispers are sounding throughout Arcavia as it becomes evident he is no closer to finding the traitor who drugged Cheryl and put a bomb in her hand. However, new information has come to light, suggesting it is not just one lone traitor in Arcavia. The Fecax have found their own traitor, who likely played a large part in the disappearance of their youngest princess.

The traitorous Fecax will be sent to Arcavia, where I will have the pleasure of torturing him as soon as I return. I glance at Amanda as she turns to walk up the stairs to our ship. As soon as *we* return.

Amanda immediately joins her friend Veronica, still choosing not to speak to me, and they make their way to their quarters. Before long, I find myself outside her door, my feet moving toward her almost without my knowledge.

I have no mating bands. There is no hint of a bond between us. Nothing compels me to her side other than the female herself, who at this moment wants nothing to do with me.

I pound on her door. Luckily, she does not have a choice.

"Who is it?"

Little brat. She is aware it is me.

"Jaret," I grind out and hear her heave a frustrated sigh.

"What do you want?"

"To talk."

"I'm busy."

I simply reach out, hitting the palm plate, and her door slides open as it recognizes my print.

Amanda leaps to her feet, and I scan the room, noticing her friend is elsewhere.

"You are such a dick!"

I ignore that. "I will give you a tour of this ship."

"I'm fine, thank you."

"I was not asking."

She throws up her hands and stalks toward me. Adrenaline pumps through my veins as I suddenly feel alive.

"Why would you think I want to talk to you? You've treated me like crap, Jaret."

"I...apologize for leaving you last night."

She is silent, and I wait while she tilts her head, scanning me with cool eyes. I know this female. She is sweet and forgiving.

"Where did you go?"

"I cannot talk about it."

She gives me a look filled with disgust and then sniffs, turning dismissively. Perhaps not as sweet and forgiving as I imagined.

Finally, she spins back, expression unreadable. "Look, we only have a few days left together before you go back to Arcavia and I stay on Earth. You're right; it's none of my business. But please don't ditch me in public like that again."

I nod, and she gives me a small smile.

"Okay, show me around the ship."

I take the day for myself, well aware my men do not need me in the control center to get us back to Earth. They are likely breathing a sigh of relief at the thought of working without my oversight.

This ship is smaller than the one we used to travel back to Arcavia. But Amanda walks with me anyway, asking questions about space travel. I show her the control center, and she stares out the wide window and into space beyond. My men are quiet, shooting me questioning glances, likely wondering why I am spending so much time with a human. Roax gives me a knowing look, and I nod, refraining from lashing out as his eyes linger on Amanda consideringly.

I take her below deck, where I explain how the ship lands.

Her eyes glaze over at one point, and I pause.

"You are tired."

"I'm sorry, Jaret. It's interesting, I swear, but you're kind of talking in a different language right now. And yeah, I got to bed late."

"I will take you back to your quarters, and you will sleep."

"You're kinda bossy, you know that?" She yawns, and I take a moment to admire her tiny white teeth. "But yeah, I guess I will take a nap."

I escort her back to her rooms, and by now, my body is tense, my fists clenching and unclenching with the need to touch her.

I should have taken Brexa up on her offer to fuck. Instant denial flashes through me. Not only is the thought of fucking Brexa repulsive, but the idea of touching any female other than Amanda is intolerable.

This is concerning.

"Jaret?" Amanda is staring at me, and I realize we have reached her room.

"Yes?"

"Are you okay?"

I shake my head, and her expression softens.

"You want to talk about it?"

I lean close, backing her against the wall. Her face is turned up toward me, and I can see the tiny dots on her nose. *Freckles.* I want to watch her sleep while I count every single one.

I groan, giving in, kissing her deeply, catching her shuddering gasp with my mouth. I want to live here, this female's body soft and pliant against mine, allowing me to kiss her like a starving male offered a feast.

When I pull away, both of us panting, I rest my forehead against hers and shiver as she runs her hand along the back of my neck.

"Tell me what's wrong."

What is wrong? The universe is wrong. This moment is wrong. My life is wrong.

"You are my mate," I finally whisper. "And I wish to the gods you were not."

Her whole body tenses, and she attempts to push away from me, but I cannot let her go, burying my face in the space that seems to have been made for me, between her shoulder and neck.

Her voice is low. "Why? Because I'm not Arcav?"

"Because if you were not my mate, I could make you mine."

Somehow, I gather every ounce of my resolve. Instead of pushing my mate back into her room, throwing her on her bed, and fucking her until we are both exhausted, I pull myself away. I do not allow myself to look back as I walk to my own quarters.

CHAPTER TWELVE

Amanda

The past two days have felt like two years. After declaring me his mate and then leaving me hanging—horny and alone—Jaret has taken great steps to stay away from me.

At one point, I felt his eyes on me as Veronica and I sat, snacking and gossiping, but I carefully avoided glancing in his direction.

I'm guessing the whole "mate" thing has been blown up in the media on Earth. I mean, sure, Varian pulled out all the stops for Harlow, but obviously being a mate isn't really such a big deal. If it were, Jaret wouldn't be acting like I'm poisonous.

We're parting ways today anyway. I ignore the ache that thought gives me. When I met Jaret, I was incredibly stressed and emotionally vulnerable, and I bonded with the first man who helped me get back to Bree. That's all it was. One day, I'll tell my grandchildren all about how their grandma made out with the hot Arcav commander.

I'm grinning as I meet Veronica's eyes, and she grins back, her whole face alight. We're currently standing in the dock, waiting to get into the smaller ship that will take us down to Earth. I'm planning to kiss the ground as soon as we land.

"Do you need help getting back to Guatemala?"

She blushes and cuts her eyes to Velax, who has been careful to avoid me ever since he helped ruin our escape plan.

"Actually, Velax is going to take me in a pod. It'll be much, much faster than flying. Plus," she says ruefully, "it's not as if I have my passport."

"I hadn't even thought of that. Do you think the other women are okay?"

Veronica nods. "They all seemed happy enough when we left. The Arcav are making sure they can find places to live and jobs if they want to stay. Otherwise, they'll return to Earth another time. You know, they're not as bad as we all think they are."

"The women?"

She elbows me and laughs. "The Arcav."

"Well, they sure beat the Grivath."

I swing my head and meet Jaret's eyes as he walks toward us. I'm so attuned to him that it's like my body is electrified whenever he's nearby.

His brows are lowered, and I'm hoping that means somewhere, in his heart of stone, he's sad to see me go. I almost snort at the thought.

"Well," I say. "I guess this is it. Thank you for everything you've done for me. I really appreciate it."

He leans forward, and for a moment, I think he's going to kiss me, but he leans down to murmur in my ear, "I'm coming with you."

"Huh?"

"You promised you would show me your element collection. Besides, I would like to see the sister you would risk your life for."

"Um, don't you need to get back to Arcavia?"

A look I can't decipher comes over his face, and then it hardens again. "I have some time."

I don't understand why he'd want to drag this out, but I shrug. "Okay."

He turns to the Arcav who will be piloting us, and the guy immediately snaps to attention. I watch as Jaret speaks to another Arcav, called Roax, who he seems to spend a lot of time with.

I wonder if Jaret has anyone close in his life. The Arcav I've seen him with have all obeyed him, but I've never seen him laughing, joking, or even seeming to have a long conversation with them. He's the most frustrating, closed-off man I've ever met.

I force my attention away. This is just like me—ending up fascinated with the wrong type of guy. I climb into the pod, and we all wait a moment until Jaret is finished and he climbs into the front passenger's seat.

He's so tall that his horns nearly brush the glass ceiling, and I smile even as I wipe my sweaty palms on my skirt. It's a gauzy material splashed in pinks and purples, and I've paired it with a neon-pink tank top. Bree would be proud.

As much as I've tried not to obsess, every moment I was away from Earth felt like it lasted hours. After announcing Bree was in a coma, my father turned his phone off. He's done a lot of shitty things over the years, but I'll never forgive him for this.

The trip in the pod takes about twenty minutes, and before I know it, I can see the hospital in front of us.

"Jaret, we can't park on the roof. A helicopter might need to land."

"We have checked for any such arrivals. We have three minutes."

The pod lands much more nimbly and more quickly than any helicopter could, and I get out while Jaret speaks with the driver. I hesitate, wringing my hands while the pod departs and Jaret takes my arm.

"I'm scared," I whisper.

He nods, and I could slap him for his matter-of-fact attitude, but then he strokes my hair back from my face, and my heart catches at the tenderness.

"Whatever happens, I promise you will get through it."

I don't think so, but I can't wait any longer, so I push open the door, and we make our way down the stairs.

"You can't be up here—whoa." A doctor rubs at her eyes as if she's imagining things, and I realize I've gotten so used to being surrounded by Arcav that I've forgotten how most humans are starstruck, terrified, and inherently wary of them. Her eyes linger on his horns as she silently steps aside, and I give her a tiny smile.

We make our way down to intensive care, and a nurse tells me Bree's room number. My whole body shudders as relief courses through it like a drug. She's still here, holding on like a fucking champion.

We make our way toward her room, and out the corner of my eye, I catch someone backing away from Jaret. I barely refrain from rolling my eyes. It's as if people think he's a serial killer or something.

My father is standing outside Bree's door.

I study him before he notices me. This man who is so focused on being "godly" yet so unwilling to be a real father that he ensured Bree and I clung to each other like we were on a life raft in the middle of the ocean.

He turns, and his eyes widen and then narrow dangerously as we approach. He would never show his rage. My father practically invented the saying "don't get mad, get even."

"What are you doing here with that *thing?*" he snaps, and I stiffen, glancing at Jaret.

Oh yeah. My father is also a bigot.

Anyone who isn't a straight white male or married to a straight white male is not to be tolerated. I'm not sure if he has technically joined Humans Against Arcav, but after searching his desk in an attempt to find leverage on him, I found evidence he's been donating to them since their inception.

"I discussed this with you," I say, voice even. "The Arcav rescued us from the Grivath. Now Jaret has brought me here even though he didn't need to. Say what you want to me, but you'll shut the hell up about him."

My father's mouth drops open and then snaps closed as Jaret unfurls himself from where he was leaning against the wall and takes a step closer.

He doesn't say a word, simply looks down at my father, who pales and steps aside. I push past him and walk in to see my sister.

Jaret

I take a moment to watch the human who has caused Amanda so much grief. He is a tall man, with the sagging jowls that humans tend to achieve with age. His eyes are hard, and the way he looks at his daughter ensures I have to fight the urge to throw him out the window. It is clear he does not appreciate what he has.

I smile. It will be that much more satisfying when I take it from him.

I follow Amanda into the small room. A woman who must be her mother sits in the corner, purple smudges beneath her eyes. She gives her daughter a small smile yet does not protest her husband's treatment of her. A steady beep sounds, and my gaze makes its way to the bed, where Amanda is already clutching her sister's hand.

Other than the beep of a machine and the wheeze of air being forced into the female's lungs, the room is silent.

Amanda has drooped like a flower, and her head lies on the bed as if she has nothing left to fight for.

This is unacceptable.

I stalk forward, my eyes drawn to the female Amanda would risk everything for. She has dark hair, while Amanda's hair is fair. Her skin is pale, but it has a slight tint as if she is usually in the sun.

I have a healer on standby, ready to check if Amanda's sister is healthy enough to be placed into stasis. I call him, ordering him to come directly to the hospital.

Then I return Varian's message.

He gets straight to his point. "Cheryl is beginning to have flashbacks. The healers believe she may regain more memories as her brain weans itself from the texain."

Cheryl is the human who was given texain—a mind-control drug more commonly known as X. The traitor chose someone from Humans Against Arcav, guaranteeing her mind would be more susceptible to suggestions that reinforced her belief Arcav are evil.

"What does she remember?"

"Not much so far. It was definitely a male, but that is not surprising. As soon as the healers give their approval, we will ask her to describe him further. But she did give us one interesting piece of information."

"Yes?"

"The Arcav had an accomplice. The human woman also remembers one phrase. Apparently, the traitor repeatedly mentioned a 'new world.'"

We are both silent for a moment as I process this. I have seen many things in my life, but one of the most disturbing was just four decades ago, when the leader of a planet named Vaire decided he did not want to give up power. Vaire was governed by a democracy, and when R'Zantai was voted out by a history-making majority, he boarded a ship. He then let loose a weapon that devastated the planet, leaving it a wasteland, with three-quarters of the population dead.

When he was finally caught for execution, R'Zantai had been raving about creating a new world.

"Do you believe the Arcav traitor has managed to get his hands on a weapon similar to the one used on Vaire?"

Varian frowns. "We cannot be too careful. I find it difficult to believe an Arcav could attain this weapon under our noses, but he may be conspiring with someone who could."

I nod. "I would like to speak with Cheryl when we arrive."

"I will talk to her healers. They are guarding her rather ferociously. I have more bad news. The Fecax traitor is dead. Someone managed to get to him before we could question him."

I grind my teeth in rage, watching Varian do the same. How are our enemies still one step ahead of us?

The healer arrives, and I meet his eyes as he hurries

down the corridor, practically salivating at the chance to potentially make medical history on Earth.

"I must go."

Amanda

I hold Bree's hand and speak to her softly, hoping she can hear me.

"I'm here now, Bree. Thank you for holding on."

I wonder if I've been selfish, insisting that she fight, even at her sickest, when I could see the exhaustion and pain written all over her face.

No. Bree loves life—every coughing, hacking, mucus-ridden minute. If this is her time to go, she did everything she could to make it this far.

I talk to her about my time in space, leaving out the scary parts. I struggle to find the words to describe the feeling of truly experiencing the magnitude of it all.

"I've never felt so small in my life, Bree. You would've loved it." I shift places, snuggling closer to her, careful of the tubes that are keeping her alive.

"You know what I remembered on the ship? That time we snuck out and went to the lake." I hear my father snort behind me and ignore him. Maybe if we'd had a little more freedom to be kids, we wouldn't have needed to continually break the rules.

"You were so excited, remember? We waited until it was two in the morning and we were sure Mom and Dad were asleep. You threw the sodium in the lake, and then we ran like hell."

Alkali metals react with water, releasing hydrogen gas.

The explosion from the sodium hitting the water made us howl like loons before we ran home, giggling the entire way.

A year later, I tried the same thing with potassium, which burst into flames as purple as the bruises on my butt after my father strapped me. The fire spread, and it was only sheer luck that a fire truck was close by, preventing a forest fire of epic proportions.

My mother moves closer, taking Bree's other hand.

"It sounds like you had quite the adventure in space," she says, gaze shattered and unfocused.

I nod, struggling to be civil. Her daughter is dying, her other daughter was abducted by aliens, and her husband is an asshole. It's not like she has an easy life.

My father moves closer, voice like a needle scraping down the back of my neck. "And how *did* you end up on that ship, Amanda?"

I frown. What exactly is he implying?

"The last thing I remember is going out for a run. Then I woke up on the Grivath ship."

"You expect us to believe that out of all the humans on this planet, *you* were unfortunate enough to be plucked from the streets?"

I know this is what he does, and yet my palms are sweating and my heart pounds with a mix of rage and anxiety. I keep my attention on my sister. Where it belongs.

"Frankly, I don't care what you think," I say, braver than I've ever been. Bree is dying. What exactly do I have left to lose?

"Careful," he says softly. "Your filthy friend won't always be around."

"Peter—" Mom says, and he silences her with a look.

I do my best to ignore him. My hatred runs deep when it comes to my father.

When I was fourteen, he kicked me out. I'd snuck out of my room to go to a party and arrived home to his fury. Bree had needed to go to the hospital in the middle of the night, and when they'd woken up, I hadn't been there. What kind of sister was I to go out and have fun when Bree was so sick?

I chose not to tell him that Bree had been planning to sneak out with me. When she'd realized she'd need to stay home and wear her percussion vest, she'd insisted I go without her so I could tell her all about it.

That night, I sat in the local park, thankful it was summer. I was terrified of everyone and everything. My heart stopped every time a homeless person shuffled by, and I imagined Bree, worrying about me from her hospital bed. The listing game was born.

When it comes to my father, I'm now a pro at ignoring his little digs. But every now and then, he slips one in like a knife between my ribs.

Cherry blossoms. Pumpkin spice lattes. Splashing in puddles. Beating Bree in Uno. Patting our neighbor Rob's golden retriever. Winning a debate competition.

"It should be you in that bed," he says, knowing exactly where to strike. He's right, of course. Bree is the kind of person who never had an unkind word to say about anyone, although the last few years with my parents have changed that. She's still the kindest person I know and has taken the cards she was dealt with acceptance and grace.

I idly wonder where Jaret has gone. Maybe he's returned to his ship. The thought twists my stomach, but I can't bring myself to think about it.

I spend the afternoon ignoring my parents and talking to my sister. Doctors come and go, speaking in low voices. Half of me wants to ask for an update, but the other half is too scared to ask.

My parents finally leave for a while, my father to get something to eat and my mother to follow him wherever he wants her to go.

I let myself fall apart.

We always knew this was a possibility. That I would outlive my twin. But if I have to bury my sister, I don't know if I'll be able to stop myself from curling up on top of her coffin and begging them to pile the dirt on top of me too.

"Please, Bree. Please don't leave me. I can't do this on my own."

I know I'm being unfair. No one wants to die from a degenerative lung disease, but I beg anyway. "You promised!"

Jaret walks in, and I give a laughing sob.

"You seem to always be around when I'm falling apart."

His icy eyes tell me he couldn't care less, that emotion is foreign to him, and somehow, it helps.

"I would like to speak with you."

I shrug, exhausted from my meltdown. "What is it?"

"I have had a healer in Arcavia look into your sister's medical file."

I wipe tears off my face as I sit up. "Why?"

"The Arcav had a similar disease to this cystic fibrosis centuries ago. We were able to eradicate it completely. I would like one of our healers to take a look at your sister. Would that be acceptable?"

I'm silent. My heart stutters in my chest, and for a moment, I can't breathe. Hope is a poisonous apple, and I'm too scared to take a bite.

Jaret waits patiently, face blank.

"Of course," I say finally, and he nods, gesturing toward the doorway, where another Arcav has appeared.

I almost laugh, but I guess it was obvious I'd agree. I

reluctantly release Bree's hand and move aside so the healer can take a look.

"My name is Heni," he tells me. "I will scan your sister, and then we can talk."

I nod and move further back, watching him as he runs his scanner over every inch of Bree's body. He examines the machines and tubes and at one point snorts with a muttered "barbaric."

"I am finished."

I'm shaking, and Jaret's cool eyes scan me before returning to Heni.

"Are you well?" Heni asks.

I nod. "Can you just give me a moment?"

I turn my back, staring out the window at the hospital parking lot. I'm terrified of whatever he'll say next. Fear is an old friend. I can cope with fear. Hope is a bitch who stabs you in the back when you least expect it.

"Okay," I say. "Give it to me."

"Your sister likely has less than one week to live. Her organs are shutting down one by one. If we can transport her to Arcavia, we have the technology to save her."

My voice trembles. "What do you mean, 'save her'? What will her life look like?"

He frowns as if he doesn't understand the question.

"Will she be able to live a normal life?"

"Oh yes. It will take her some time to recover, and she may need to take medication for a few months, but there is no reason to believe she will not live a full and happy life."

I feel like I have been given the moon, the sun, and the stars. I meet Jaret's eyes, and I know if this man asked me to cut off my right arm and hand it to him in this moment, I'd do it.

"Let's make it happen."

My sister is going to live. No...she's going to thrive.

"What's going on here?"

I whirl as my parents reappear.

"We can save Bree's life," I tell them, and my mom closes her eyes, sinking into a chair.

"How, exactly?" My father's tone is belligerent, and I want to hit him for shitting all over this opportunity.

"We will put her in something called stasis," Heni replies. "This shuts down all functions, essentially 'pausing' her body until she can be attended to in Arcavia."

"Arcavia? You're not taking my daughter off this planet."

"She'll die!" My voice is a screech, and my mother looks up, fire in her eyes for the first time in years.

My father whirls on me, his face dangerously red. At that moment, I want nothing more than for him to have a heart attack so I can watch him writhe on the floor, the way he's happy to watch Bree suffer.

"Better for her to live a godly life and ascend to heaven than to surround herself with demons." He points at Jaret's horns, and I let out a stunned laugh.

"You're a fucking idiot," I say wondrously.

"Watch your mouth."

"We don't believe in *your* God," I say as his eyes widen. "So you can take your narrow-mindedness and your hypocrisy and suck it."

He slaps me so hard my face whips to the side and tears immediately fill my eyes. I have a flashback to the Grivath hitting me on the ship and almost laugh even as I suppress the urge to sob.

Jaret goes eerily still. Then he *moves.*

One moment my father is standing in front of me, hand raised, fury in his eyes, and the next, Jaret has shoved him through a wall.

CHAPTER THIRTEEN

Jaret

The human male chokes as I hold him, my hand wrapped around his throat. I study him dispassionately. What kind of planet is this, where males raise their hands to females with no repercussions?

He is turning a deep purple as humans surround me. I should not have allowed this man to strike Amanda. Never did I imagine he would hit her fragile face. I was unprepared. But I will never be again.

"Jaret." A soft hand is stroking my neck. "Please let him go. I think he got the point."

I consider this. The male has spoken harshly to every female, particularly the woman who is begging me to let him go. But if I kill him, she may be upset with me.

I release my hand slowly, and the male slumps to the ground.

"Thank you," Amanda says.

"Do it," a hoarse voice says.

We all turn to Amanda's mother, who is holding Brianna's hand while stroking her face. She turns, tears dripping onto her daughter like rain.

"If you can save her, do it. Make her live."

"No." The word is garbled, but no one pays attention to the man who would rather his daughter die than be given a chance somewhere other than Earth.

"Mom?"

"Look after your sister. And yourself. I know you'll fight for her. The way I should've fought for you both."

Amanda's head is high, and her eyes spark with emotion. "I've got this, Mom."

I nod at Heni, who immediately begins making preparations. There is no question—now that her sister will be taken to Arcavia, Amanda will be returning with me.

I leave the room to make arrangements.

I am not softhearted. I do not do good deeds simply to do them. I need to bring Amanda back to Arcavia—in spite of the fact we cannot complete our mating. The best way to do this is to take her sister with me.

If I were a better man, I would feel guilt at my actions. I justify them with the thought that Amanda was willing to attempt an escape into space simply to be near her sister. Of course she would be willing to travel back to Arcavia to see her life saved.

The feelings Amanda inspires in me are dangerous. Without preparing for this outcome, I could have gotten to the point I was like Varian—obsessed with his mate and instantly responding to the slightest change in her mood.

Thankfully, I prevented this.

If Amanda were to die, I would be unhappy. But I would not be tempted to follow her. This is a theory that no Arcav has tested before, but I believe that preventing a full mating is crucial.

If she were my mate in truth and something happened to her, I would soon follow. The Arcav would be left without a commander, just as they need me the most as a leader against the Grivath. I will not leave this universe until the Grivath general who tortured and killed my mother is writhing in agony and begging to die.

Amanda

I pack up my element collection, which I've kept with Bree's things. Heni is speaking with Bree's doctors to discuss her transport to the ship, where she'll be put in stasis.

The worst night of my life—a night spent on a Grivath ship—has led to the best moment I could ever imagine. Saving my sister's life.

I smile at Jaret as he enters, and his eyes scan me before he gives me an absent nod. His mind seems to have as much uncharted territory as space itself.

And I want to map all of it.

Bree will be transported to the ship in a helicopter, since she needs to remain hooked up to all her various machines until the Arcav can take over. It all feels surreal, and I wish she could open her eyes and tell me I'm doing the right thing.

Jaret and I make our way up to the roof, where Bree is loaded onto the helicopter with Heni and a few human doctors. They have been remarkably helpful, and her primary human doctor shakes my hand as he turns to get into the helicopter.

"Good luck to you and your sister," he says. "Perhaps this

will pave the way for greater Arcav and human cooperation in the medical field."

I nod, and it hits me. This is truly groundbreaking. Sure, the Arcav have shared technology to help our planet. But as far as I'm aware, this is the first time they've saved a human's life without something in it for them. Maybe this means they're opening up to the possibility of helping us conquer the diseases that have impacted so many humans for so long.

The helicopter takes off, and Jaret gestures for me to get in the pod as it arrives. I take a seat, mentally saying goodbye to my planet as we fly over the city. There was no question and no discussion. If Bree is going to Arcavia, I obviously am too. One day, we'll return to our lives. But we need to save Bree's life first.

I study Jaret, who is so remote and yet somehow always seems to know what I need. I feel lost, untethered and can't stop second-guessing myself. I know deep down this is what Bree would want. The chance to fight. The opportunity to see space. A life. But I'm also well aware she has signed a Do Not Resuscitate form.

We had a glorious fight about that.

Jaret has arranged for the smaller ship to land, and we beat the helicopter there. Velax still looks wary and slightly ashamed when I meet his eyes, and I smile at him. Let's face it: Veronica and I would probably have died if we'd managed to take that ship. Now the future is bright again.

We watch the helicopter land, and Bree is unloaded. The Arcav take over, transporting her into the ship as Heni finishes speaking to her human doctors.

Jaret's cold eyes meet mine, and I nod. Time to go.

He takes me straight to the medi-center, where Bree will soon be put into stasis. The ground shifts almost imperceptibly beneath my feet, indicating we're already traveling to the main ship.

Heni looks up. "I must warn you. This is not an enjoyable process to watch. Your sister will appear as if she is dead. You may wish to leave for this."

I shake my head. "I'm staying."

Jaret makes a movement beside me as if he's about to protest, and I narrow my eyes at him. He frowns but gestures for Heni to continue.

It's fucking brutal.

The machines have to be removed in a specific order, and there's one excruciating moment where Bree's chest lies flat and one long, steady beep announces her heart is no longer beating. It takes everything in me to not leap forward in a frantic attempt to reconnect the medical devices even though I have no understanding of how they work.

Getting ready for prom with Bree. Laughing as we dance to nineties hits. Divulging our secret crushes under the covers.

I hold it together. I'm done with crying. Now my sister gets to live, and we get to have incredible, amazing, glorious lives. We'll meet men who love us and would never try to kill our spirit like our father did to our mother. We'll both have kids, who will be best friends. And we'll make the most of every single second we have on this crazy ride called life. Together.

CHAPTER FOURTEEN

Jaret

Amanda is quiet, and something inside me refuses to let her return to her room alone. Once we have docked on the ship that will return us to Arcavia, I bring her to a small sitting room near her quarters. I am hoping the lack of a bed nearby will help me restrain myself. Will help me keep my hands off her.

"Tell me about your life before you were taken," I say to distract her.

"Well...we grew up in DC—the city we just left. My mom stayed at home, while my father worked. Bree was really sick as a kid, so one of them needed to be available full-time. I think Bree has always felt bad about that, but I dunno if my father would've let Mom work anyway." She sighs.

"Your father makes you unhappy."

Amanda shifts, idly playing with the strap from her bag. "You know, I don't think he's truly evil, not deep down. He's just the most selfish person I've ever met. I once heard him tell my mom that God had given Bree CF to test *his* faith," she says, voice dripping with bitterness. "When you guys invaded, it was like something inside him broke. He became worse than ever, sure that the Arcav had to be demons. He was nearly fired when he began telling people the world was ending. He's a conspiracist and barely believes in science."

She takes a deep breath and then slowly lets it out. "When someone believes something despite all evidence to the contrary, there's no reasoning with them. I know that now. My therapist called it cognitive dissonance."

"I am sorry."

She shrugs. "He is who he is. Bree coped with it like she does everything—she tried to find humor in it. I coped with it by ignoring it and becoming obsessed with Bree's health for a while. I lost two jobs because I refused to leave her side when she got really sick." She grins. "Don't tell her that. I told her I quit."

"You are dedicated to your sister."

"I'm pretty sure I need her more than she needs me. Bree has always been the stronger one, while I tend to cling. Unfortunately, I couldn't trust our parents to make the best possible decisions for her, so I felt like I always needed to be there."

She looks away, and I almost growl. This female does not consider herself to be strong?

"You have shown incredible strength time and time again. I have heard about how you taunted the Grivath in an effort to find a way to escape. Not to mention your dangerous plan to steal my ship. Your decisions may be foolhardy, but they are also brave."

Amanda gives me a soft smile. "Thanks."

I can tell she does not truly believe me, and I want to shake her.

She meets my eyes. "You don't have any siblings?"

I frown at the change of subject but allow it. For now.

"No. Arcav have low fertility rates. But I believe my parents would have been ecstatic if they had been able to have another child."

She nods.

"What are you thinking?" I ask.

"Are we ever going to talk about the mating thing?"

She grins at me, her tiny nose wrinkling, and I almost curse. Is it any wonder I want nothing more than to be inside this female? I feel a bolt of shame hit me for my attitude toward humans before this. Amanda has shown me that while they may not be as evolved as other species, they love just as fiercely.

Out of all the females in the universe, this one is mine.

I groan, lean over, and fist her long hair, pulling her close so I can kiss her. She smells sweet and female and opens for me, submitting to me.

She knows she is mine.

I kiss my way down her neck, and her hands clench in my hair, brushing my horns. I fight for control, grinding my teeth as she gasps and writhes against me as I nibble on a particularly sensitive spot near her shoulder.

I push her further back into the sofa and pull her thin top down, revealing lace.

Her nipples pop out, and I stare, entranced. Her breasts are perfect. Pear-shaped and plump, with hard pink nipples. She shivers and begins to flush at my stare, attempting to cross her arms.

I catch them. "No hiding."

"Stop staring!" She squirms.

"You are beautiful." I lean close, nuzzling her. She has

more dots—freckles—across her chest, and I brush kisses over them, enjoying her soft gasps and sighs.

Her head rolls back, languid, and then she groans as I take her nipple in my mouth, tugging while I keep my eyes on her face.

I've never been this hard.

I move down, kneeling between her thighs. Amanda is wearing another gauzy jewel-colored skirt designed to make me lose my mind. I flip it up, nuzzling between her thighs, and slice her thin underwear off with one claw.

I run my lips over her sex before sliding my tongue along her, flicking her clit. I'm careful with my claws, which refuse to retract, something that has never happened to me before.

Amanda moans, her hands tugging at my horns. I press her into the sofa, spread her legs further apart, and plunge deeper into her, still stroking her clit.

"Jesus," she gasps. "For a guy who just learned how to kiss, you sure are good at that."

I chuckle against her, enjoying her sweetness on my tongue.

"Don't stop," she orders, and I obey, determined to feel her come. She shrieks as her entire body tenses, thighs shaking as her orgasm slams through her, and I groan as her cunt clenches on my tongue.

I'm moving up her body, fumbling as I loosen my pants, desperate to slide into her.

And then I freeze.

She is spread on the sofa, blonde hair a tangled mess, body flushed a soft pink, and bright skirt still flipped up. Her amber eyes are heavy lidded and satisfied. She looks like a rainbow.

Until I see her wrists.

Black mating bands cover her fair skin, and horror, triumph, and regret war inside me at the sight. I pull her skirt back down, closing my eyes as I shove my dick back in my pants.

It screams at me to keep going, to make this female mine.

I ignore it and grit my teeth as I step back from Amanda, loathing myself for the confusion in her eyes as she stares at me.

"What's wrong?"

I gesture to her wrists. "This was a mistake."

Amanda

I fumble for my tank top, pulling it over my head as Jaret turns away.

What the hell? I take a moment to stare at my wrists, not sure how to feel. If they were from someone who actually wanted to be with me, I'd probably be elated.

"What's wrong?"

He turns back, and his eyes are blank as if someone has turned them off, extinguishing the light inside him. I want to shake him. His light could brighten the whole sky if he let it.

"I am...with someone else."

He's pulling out my heart and setting fire to it.

"It's that Arcav woman from the wedding, isn't it?"

"It is not what you think. I must appear to be with her for reasons outside my control."

"Reasons like what?"

Her incredible hair? Amazing boobs?

I snort. "I thought mating was everything to you guys. What possible reason could you have for giving up on us before we even begin?"

"I will never have a true mating. Arcav matings are weaknesses that should not be tolerated. With mating and a love match, Arcav are incapable of living full lives if their mate should die."

"That's what you're worried about? Being alone if your mate dies?" My voice is strangled.

He looks away. "When my mother died, my father lasted three days before he took his own life, leaving me alone."

My heart hurts for the little boy who lost a mother and then a father who wasn't strong enough to face life without her. But he's no longer a kid. Jaret has pushed people away his whole life, determined not to be vulnerable. Refusing to risk being left alone again.

"I'm sorry that happened to you, Jaret. But why does that mean we can't have a long and happy life together?"

He takes my hand. "I do not want to hurt you. But this will never happen for us. I am sorry."

"You're *breaking* my heart." My voice cracks, and I shake off his hand.

"You will still have a good life on Arcavia."

"Please," I beg. "Just explain why you're with her. Do you love her?"

One day, I'll look back on this moment as the one where I threw my dignity out the window.

"Brexa is helping me find the Grivath that killed my mother. In return, I will stay by her side."

And in her bed? I don't even want to ask. He doesn't speak fondly of the Arcav woman, and I've never seen his eyes heat when he looks at her. Not even a dull imitation of the way they burn when he looks at me.

He looks at Brexa as if he barely tolerates her. I know because it's the same way my father often looks at my mother. It's that thought that makes me try one last time.

I take a deep breath. "Do you think I don't understand the need to get revenge? I know what it's like to love someone with everything you have."

"Your sister will live. Thanks to me. Remember that."

"I do! Is that what you want? For me to live my life on my knees in gratitude? Is that why you did it?"

He raises an eyebrow. "Did you think I did it out of the goodness of my heart? Have you *met* me? I told you I could never make you happy. Why did you not listen?"

I smile, and it's bitter. "You're right. I should've listened."

Men 101, right? When a guy tells you who they are, pay attention.

"This doesn't need to be difficult. You can live your life, and I can live mine."

In that moment, I hate him. I hate him so much I would destroy his life if I could. My mind flashes back to the moment I first saw him, outside the bars of my cage on the Grivath ship. Those cold, dead eyes staring at me dispassionately. I knew this man could damage me. But I didn't think he could ruin me so completely.

"I think you should stay the fuck away from me."

"That's not how it works, mate. You need to be close so that I can stay focused."

"Get your focus elsewhere."

CHAPTER FIFTEEN

Amanda

The return to Arcavia seems to take forever, but I know it's just a few days. I avoid Jaret like he's contagious, sticking to my room and ignoring him. After one attempt to talk to me—when I sat on my bed and stared at the door silently while he knocked—he didn't try again.

I wish I could summon some fury. But I'm too hurt. The black mating bands on my wrists should signify I'm wanted, needed. But Jaret has made it clear that's not the case at all. If I could, I'd turn back time and remove them for good. Jaret has decided they will never turn the pretty silver of Harlow's bands, and I'll never show them off by choosing a matching dress the way Jen did for the wedding.

They'll stay black forever, branding me as unwanted, unnecessary, yet taken.

I gather my element collection, the only thing I truly own. Even my clothes are borrowed, although it seems like the Arcav have more than enough to go around.

For now, my only goal is to stay with Bree until she's no

longer sick. She's currently being unloaded off the ship and into a larger pod than any I've seen before. I follow her off the ship, and Jaret walks silently next to me. Heni gestures for me to sit in the back of the pod next to Bree, who is still lying in a glass chamber filled with some kind of gas.

I can't forget that without Jaret, Bree would be dead right now.

"Thank you for arranging for her to be brought back," I mutter, making eye contact for the first time since the mating bands appeared.

His dead eyes blink, and then he turns away. "You are welcome."

We're taken to the medi-center, which already has a room prepared for Bree. Her new bed is large, and against one wall, a plush sofa and two armchairs sit, with a small coffee table in front of them. The walls are a soft blue, and several lamps are scattered around. It's quiet but not spooky, and while there are some machines I've never seen before, the room feels comforting, not cold and sterile like the hospital on Earth.

Heni has been with us the entire time, answering any questions I've had about the process. Basically, stasis has frozen the clock. Bree will be just as sick as she was on Earth, but here, the Arcav will immediately begin treating her.

Another Arcav enters, smiling at us.

"You must be Amanda," he says. "My name is Brin, and I'll be taking over your sister's care."

He has an air of confidence, and my intuition immediately tells me I can trust him with my sister's life.

"You made the right decision," he assures me. "After her treatment, Brianna will wake up, feeling better than she likely ever has."

I blink back tears. I've been told this, of course, but the confirmation is exactly what I need.

Soon, soon I'll hear Bree's voice. I'll introduce her to Harlow and her friends. We'll explore Arcavia, and the next time she's on a spaceship, she'll be fully conscious and able to enjoy it.

"Can I stay?"

Brin nods. "We need to take her out of stasis and begin treatment. I would prefer for you to leave for that, as it can be a difficult process to witness. Perhaps you could get something to eat? As soon as the treatment has begun, you may return and wait with her for as long as you like. We will have another bed brought in here so you may sleep."

"Thank you."

I hesitate, taking one last look at my sister, frozen and lifeless. I walk outside, slumping into one of the armchairs that line the hall.

Jaret sits beside me. "Will you come and eat?"

"I'm not hungry."

He simply nods, and I turn away, gazing at the light-gray wall in front of me. "You can leave. I'm fine."

I can *feel* his frown as he clears his throat. "I will stay."

"I'd rather be alone."

Silence. I glance at him, and his expression darkens as he stares back at me. A muscle in his jaw pulses, but he finally nods, turns, and walks away.

I don't know how much time passes while I wait, but Brin eventually comes out and allows me to reenter the room. Bree's chest rises and falls—without a ventilator—and she looks like she's sleeping.

"When will she wake up?"

Brin smiles. "It could be a few hours; it could be a few

weeks. It depends how fast her body responds to the treatment."

I nod and sit next to Bree, taking her hand, like I have so many times before.

"Let me know if you need anything. I will come back to check her in a few hours." He turns to go, and I jump up, throwing my arms around him.

"Thank you," I say. "You don't know how much this means to me."

He simply smiles. "You are most welcome."

I sit and stare at my sister for hours, letting my mind wander. I hope Mom is okay. I should have asked her to come to Arcavia with us, but I know she would never leave my father. And he'd never go near a spaceship.

"You know, sometimes I'd wish I was the one who was sick," I tell Bree. "And other times, I'd see you gasping for air and coughing up mucus and feel so fucking grateful I wasn't. Of course, then I'd feel guilty for days, barely able to look at you." I let out a small laugh. Bree knew. She knew exactly how I thought.

My sister and I have never had what you'd call a normal relationship. We never fought. There was no silent treatment, no screaming at each other, no emotional manipulation.

We didn't have the time.

When it comes to life and death, needles and nurses, and watching your twin struggle for each breath, shit gets real. Bree had to make the best possible decisions under the worst possible circumstances, with little emotional support from our parents. Petty squabbles over boys and clothes didn't compare.

My sister had to be just the right level of sick. Sick enough to qualify for a transplant, which is pretty fucking sick, but not sick enough that she wouldn't be able to get through the transplant itself.

It's a thin line to walk.

"We're due for a really big, overdramatic fight one day, sister mine. Complete with pouting and the silent treatment." I snort at the thought.

I tell her about Jaret, about the mating bands, and even about his skills with his tongue. I'll repeat all this to her when she wakes up, but for now, I want her to know she's not alone.

I doze fitfully in my chair, my head on Bree's bed. Brin has another Arcav bring in a small bed, which he pulls close to Bree's so I can still hold her hand. A few hours later, I wake up and whisper to her some more.

"You would've been cheering for Mom if you could've seen her. She finally stood up to him, Bree. And she did it for you. God, I bet he's making her pay for it too."

I snuggle closer. "You know, you always used to ask me what element I was. I liked to think of myself as beryllium. Strong, with a high melting temperature and resistant to corrosion. Of course, it's also expensive and highly poisonous." I laugh softly.

"But maybe I'm really molybdenum. It's able to withstand incredible stress for long periods of time at high temperatures. Maybe that's my superpower."

Bree groans. "You idiot. You're oxygen. You've always been oxygen."

I freeze as her hoarse voice hits me. Am I dreaming?

She clears her throat, and I lift my head as she continues to mutter. "Sure, carbon is the foundation of all life. But oxygen is the fuel that makes that life possible." She opens her eyes.

"I like it," I say around the lump in my throat. "The gas

gives life. The liquid threatens it." I curl into my sister as she wraps her arms around me.

And I let myself fall apart.

Jaret

Brin informs me Bree is awake. I have almost visited many times over the past two days, but I am not welcome. Amanda does not want to see me, and I cannot blame her.

It is for the best.

I find Varian in his quarters, where he now spends most of his time. The sound of retching reaches my ears as I walk in, and I raise an eyebrow at Varian, who is hovering outside the bathroom door.

"Harlow has ordered me to stay outside when this happens," he says, glaring at the door as if it has personally offended him.

"Is she no better?"

"Each time the healers find a new solution, it lasts only a few days. The day after our weeding, the sickness returned. There are human drugs; however, Harlow does not want to risk using them, as the baby is half Arcav."

Harlow opens the door. "Wedding," she says around the toothbrush in her mouth, "not weeding. How's Amanda doing?" she asks me. "I heard about her sister."

She retreats to rinse her mouth, and I wait until she returns. As soon as she crosses the doorway, Varian scoops her into his arms and places her gently on the sofa.

"She is...fine," I say when she looks at me expectantly.

"Uh-huh," she says, narrowing her eyes at me. "Fine, huh?"

I ignore her and turn to Varian just as the door slams open.

Harlow jumps and yelps at the unexpected intrusion, her head whipping toward the door.

Varian growls, claws extended as he stalks toward the young Arcav who dared interrupt him and startled his mate.

"I—I am sorry, Your Majesty, but it is an emergency. You have not answered your communicator, so I was sent instead."

"It's okay," Harlow says, smiling at the Arcav, who has likely just joined the armed forces and is currently close to trembling.

"Name," Varian says.

"Nevi, Your Majesty."

Harlow gets to her feet and brings him a glass of water. Nevi stares at her and then the water in astonishment while Varian walks into his bedroom before returning with his communicator.

Varian's eyes close, and Harlow clutches at her chest, likely feeling the deep despair that is currently written all over his face. My wrists burn as if punishing me for the bond I will never have with my own mate.

Varian's voice is ice when he finally speaks.

"The Fecax royal family. They are all dead." Varian's face is shuttered, his eyes pained.

Tears slip down Harlow's face.

"I'm so sorry, Varian. I know you were close to Xiax."

"You never met him," Varian says. "I am sorry for that. I was too jealous to allow him close to you."

"Shh." Harlow raises her hand to his face and cups his cheek, and I turn to the window, allowing them a moment.

"They were found dead in their beds. The Grivath could not have gotten past our defense or entered the Fecax shields. They were killed by someone they knew and trusted."

"Oh my God." Harlow is shaking, and Varian pulls her close.

"Jaret." Varian's tone is hard, his rage quickly replacing sadness. I nod in approval. Rage is fuel that will get results.

"What is the current status of the search for the Fecax princess?" He closes his eyes. "The Fecax queen," he says hoarsely.

"We know she was kidnapped, but we are still unsure where she was taken. It was not the Grivath but likely one of their allies looking to win favor or strike a deal. A ship was sighted refueling in Ecron, with rumors of a small Fecax female onboard."

"Talis cannot be spared right now. He is already on the way to Fecax with Methi. Who do you recommend to take charge of the search?"

I frown. The Fecax princess is now queen. Her entire family has been slaughtered, and the already impressive bounty on her head will now be astronomical.

"Roax," I say.

Varian nods. "Send him now."

CHAPTER SIXTEEN

Amanda

I spend two days hanging out with Bree. She gradually gets her color back, and for the first time in her life, her sentences aren't peppered with small coughs. She's sitting up, grinning as I tell her about how I tried to escape the Arcav ship, when Harlow walks in.

"Wow," Bree says. "I know that face."

Harlow grins, but she's pale, with dark circles under her eyes. Worse, she looks like she's lost weight since the last time I saw her.

"I could say the same thing. It's great to finally see you awake." Harlow hands me a bag. "I brought you guys some clothes. I know they have stuff here, but I figured you might want more variety."

"That's so nice," Bree says. "Thanks."

Eve walks in. "Nathan will stay outside," she says to Harlow and then reaches out to shake Bree's hand. "It's nice to meet you."

"What's going on?" I ask.

Harlow sighs. "The Fecax royal family was just murdered. Varian has let me be pretty relaxed with the whole guard thing up until now, but shit just got serious." She gestures toward her stomach, where a tiny bump is beginning to show.

"I'm so sorry," I murmur, and Harlow nods.

"Anyway, how are you guys? How are you feeling?" she asks Bree.

"I'm feeling amazing." Bree grins. "I just...can't imagine what our world would be like if we had these types of treatments, you know?"

Harlow nods. "I totally get it. And believe me, I want to move in that direction too. It's just taking some time. Actually," she says, turning to me, "that's kind of what I wanted to talk to you about."

"Oh yeah?"

"What are your plans now? Will you guys stay in Arcavia?"

I freeze. I have no idea. I guess we don't really have to, unless I consider the mating bands.

I hold out my wrists, and her mouth drops open.

"Wow. Uh, how do you feel about it?"

I gesture toward the chair, and Harlow plops down while I slump on Bree's bed. Eve leans against the wall, giving my wrists a sympathetic glance.

"Not too great, to be honest. Jaret has no intention of actually being my mate. But I don't know if he'll let me leave."

Harlow jolts out of her chair and begins pacing, obviously furious. "This is just like him to want the best of both worlds."

She points to my wrists. "Black mating bands simply mean that you're taken. Kind of like an engagement ring, I guess. The true bond comes once they turn silver—when both sides accept the mating. Jaret obviously wants to keep you close enough he won't risk going crazy but for whatever reason, doesn't want to actually have a mate."

Eve snorts. "What a dick."

I'm depressed, but for some weird reason, I still feel the need to defend Jaret. "He says he's focused on avenging his mom's murder."

Harlow just shakes her head.

"I'm sure you guys will work it out," she says. "But in the event you want to help change a few things, I have an offer for you."

I raise a brow, gesturing for her to continue.

"I'm in the process of putting together an Earth Council. Basically, it's a way for us humans to negotiate with the Arcav. You used to write policy in DC, right?"

My mouth drops open. Harlow waits patiently while I find my words.

"Sure, but I was trying to get more bike lanes, not campaigning for human rights."

Harlow waves her hand dismissively. "We've created a team of experts, and we're looking for representatives from every country on Earth. There's more than enough work to do. But we also need people who have actually interacted with the Arcav, and people who have some skin in the game." She gestures toward my wrists.

"Wow." I look at Bree, who grins and gives me a thumbs-up. "I'd love to."

"Excellent." Harlow smirks like she expected no other answer, and I raise an eyebrow.

"Does anyone ever say no to you?"

Eve rolls her eyes. "It's better to just go along with what she suggests. Case in point: I'm teaching a female self-defense class tomorrow if you guys want to come along?"

Bree wriggles a little. "I've always wanted to do one of those! I'm allowed out of here later today, so we'll be there. I, uh, might be a little out of shape though," she says.

"Girl, three days ago you were dying." Harlow laughs. "Cut yourself a break. I'm going too, although if I'm as nauseous as I've been recently, I'll be cheering you guys on from the sidelines. Oh, one more thing." She sits on the corner of Bree's bed and looks at us. "I've arranged for you two to have your own quarters near ours. You'll have more than enough space, and it'll give you guys a chance to hang out."

"God. How are you so nice?" Bree asks wonderingly.

Eve snorts. "Ask the last Grivath who attempted to take her somewhere she didn't want to go."

A knock sounds on the door, and we all turn as it opens. Jaret meets my eyes and then turns to Bree.

"I am Jaret. It is good to see you awake."

She smiles. "It's good to be awake. Thank you for everything you did to make it happen."

He nods and turns to me. "I would like to talk to you."

I take a moment to think about it. Now that I'm not feeling so fragile and no longer worried about Bree, it might be a good idea to clear the air.

I glance at Bree, who is already deep in conversation with Harlow and Eve, and then I nod, stepping outside with him.

It...hurts to be near him. I can barely look at the guy who brought me so much pleasure only to immediately follow it with so much pain.

Jaret is silent as he leads me down the hall and into another room similar to Bree's. He gestures for the chair, and I sit, staring up at the face I currently see over and over in my dreams.

He's so untouchable, eyes blank as he stares at me. And yet I know he feels. I've seen those eyes hot with lust as he pushed my thighs apart and dark with pain when he spoke about his mother.

"I would like to be...friends."

"Friends?"

He nods, and I frown. I don't want to be his friend. I want to be his everything.

"Why?"

He scowls. "What do you mean, why?"

"You told me you have no friends, Jaret," I say. "So why would you want to be friends with me? Would it have anything to do with the idea of keeping your mate close, your *friends* closer?"

"I have explained to you why we cannot be together as mates. Yes, I would like to see you regularly so that I do not risk my focus during this time. Already I am quick to rage."

I shake my head, so damn disappointed. I don't know what I was hoping to hear, but it wasn't this. And yet I can't simply turn him away. He saved Bree's life. Like it or not, I owe him.

"I don't want to be your friend," I tell him. "But I will agree to a certain amount of contact each week so that you can keep your *focus.*"

He narrows his eyes at me, and his fists clench. Ah. Maybe he *is* beginning to lose his precious focus. But what he considers losing focus, I consider his wall of ice breaking down.

"You blame me for choosing to continue my search for my mother's killer."

I get to my feet. "I don't. But I do blame you for choosing it over an opportunity to live a full life."

He steps closer. "I have seen how much you love your sister. Can you tell me you would act any differently if she were taken from you by an enemy?"

"After a century of revenge and bitterness? If heaven exists, and I got to see her again, my sister would kick my ass for wasting my life on vengeance instead of trying to be happy."

"Vengeance *will* make me happy!" he roars, and I smile sadly.

"I'm sorry you believe that."

He rubs a hand over one of his horns, suddenly looking so frustrated that I almost laugh. It's moments like these, when I see glimpses of who he truly is underneath, that leave me desperate for more.

"I do not understand you," he says.

"I know. I don't understand you either."

He growls, reaches out, and drags me to him. I land against his chest with a thump, opening my mouth in surprise, and he takes advantage, cupping the back of my neck and attacking my mouth.

God, he can kiss.

He reaches for my top, only removing his mouth from me for the split second it takes to pull it over my head. My skirt and bra are next, falling to the floor as he moves me even closer, surrounding me with his strong arms, his scent. I wonder if he's getting a crick in his neck from leaning down so far to kiss me, but the next second, he's lifting me into his arms and deepening our kiss as I gasp at the sudden movement.

My groan is completely undignified as he lays me on the bed, following me down, still kissing me. One of his hands moves down to play with my nipple while the other begins a steady rhythm as he strokes my clit.

"I'm so mad at you," I growl as my nails dig into his shoulders.

He simply pulls away, right as I'm on the cusp of something amazing, and I can only manage a garble of filthy words as I balance on the precipice.

"You have a dirty mouth," he says, and then, without any further warning, he's pressing at my entrance.

I have a moment to wonder if he'll even fit, and then he's filling me up, so perfectly, so *completely* that I wonder why I've ever wasted time with any other man.

And then he's thrusting, his eyes glowing as he stares down at me, and my own eyes roll as I gasp out curses. I wrap my legs around his waist, and he leans down, taking my lips as he moves within me, hitting a spot that has every muscle in my body cramping with tension.

He grinds against my clit, and I see stars. But it's his low growl that sends me over, my climax tearing through me as I shudder. Jaret thrusts twice more before he buries his head in my neck and floods me with heat.

We're both silent and panting, and I feel the moment he realizes what he's done, his body turning to iron.

He pulls out of me, shaking, and I mourn the loss of his heat against my body. And then I jolt as his arm whips out, grabbing my wrist and pulling it close. I don't need the mating bond to feel the immense relief that pours from him when he sees that my mating bands are still black.

I shake off his hand, pushing at him. "Get off, get off!"

He clenches his jaw but obeys, moving away from the bed. I point at my skirt and bra, lying on the floor, and he hands them to me before turning around, as if giving me privacy.

My hands are shaking, and I fight back tears. One day, I'll make Jaret feel as small as I do right now. I'm not proud of it, but my number one goal is to make him pay.

Jaret

I have...made a misstep.

I turn back around as Amanda hops off the bed and almost flinch as I meet her eyes.

Previously, when she looked at me, I would see a range of emotions. Yearning, frustration, indulgence, confusion. Now her eyes are as hard and cold as those I see in the mirror each day.

I should not have lost control. And yet my hands clench as I fight the urge to roll her beneath me again.

Her eyes pass over me dismissively.

"That will never happen again," she says.

"You are right. It was a mistake."

A mistake because this small female makes me dream of a better life, one where I spend the majority of my time bringing her pleasure.

I *feel* her pain at my words as if I have been stabbed in the gut, and I check her mating bands one more time. She glowers at me as I glance at her wrists and then moves, ducking around my body and darting out the door.

"I hate you," she hisses.

I slump in the chair when she is gone, her scent remaining long after she has left. My mother's face swims in front of my eyes, her soft smile and kind eyes giving me reassurance. She would have loved Amanda.

"What is your goal in life, son?"

"Avenge my parents."
"And how will you avenge them?"
"I will not stop until every last Grivath is dead."

I get to my feet. Yes, my mother would have loved Amanda. She would have introduced her to her friends, shown off her garden, and told her stories of her life in the armed forces. But she will never get that chance. Because she is dead.

Amanda

Bree and I spend the day exploring Arcavia. She's still recovering, so we walk slowly, but she's also full of energy, excitement, and gratitude to be alive. Bree is the perfect person to be around considering how I feel right now.

"Stop thinking about him."

I sigh. "Get in the pod. We need to go to Eve's self-defense class."

Harlow has arranged for us to have a driver, although Bree has declared she'll be driving a pod herself by the end of the month. We haven't talked about returning to Earth, and from the way Bree is gushing about Arcavia, that talk may not happen.

"A good workout is just what you need. You can take all that anger out on a punching bag."

I nod. I *am* angry. In fact, I'm furious—not just at Jaret but at myself for being so stupid. My initial flash of vengeance has given way to a boiling anger and occasional depression. I know better than to try to change a man. Jaret told me who he was, explained his priorities, and let me know in no uncertain terms we would never be together.

And then I slept with him anyway. Because I wanted to know what it would be like to feel him moving inside me.

Well, now you know. Are you happy?

I blow out a breath. I've gotten through life by focusing on the good stuff. By being relentlessly optimistic and, okay, probably annoyingly positive.

With Jaret, I can't play the listing game. His face drowns out everything else. If I let him, Jaret will erase my rainbows and stomp on my sunflowers. He'll wreck me more thoroughly than anything else ever could.

So I won't let him.

Bree points out the palace, which shoots into the sky like a glass arrowhead. She's absolutely entranced with Arcavia, but I see Jaret everywhere. Each time I see a pair of horns—which appear at every turn—my heart stops.

I need to get my head in the game, and I tune back into Bree as we land, and the driver directs us to the spot where we're meeting Eve.

"Wow, check this place out," Bree says.

It's pretty damn impressive. The stadium is packed with gym equipment, and both Arcav and humans are working out, doing everything from racing up the long ropes dangling from the ceiling, to lifting weights.

"Ooh," Bree whispers as a well-built human guy walks past, ripping his shirt off and bundling it in his hand. "I think I'm gonna like it here."

I smirk, and we turn as a voice calls my name.

"There you guys are! I hope you've had a good day. The other girls are already warming up. We've taken our own corner away from the craziness." Harlow gestures at the testosterone around us and bursts out laughing at Bree's fake pout.

"Don't worry, girl, there'll be plenty of time for that later."

We join the warm-up, where Eve has around twenty other women jogging in place. Nathan has followed Harlow, and he waves to Eve as he takes a seat.

"Hey, Small."

Eve scowls, and I raise an eyebrow at Harlow.

"Long story," she says, puffing out a breath as we switch to high knees. "But Korva declared that Eve was *small* in front of about fifty people. Word got around, and now that's her new nickname."

I wince. "Yikes."

"Yeah. Her revenge will likely be brutal. I've told her to just embrace it, but let's face it—it's not the greatest nickname for the only female on my guard."

"Do you two chatterboxes want to do some push-ups, or are you ready to listen?" Eve's voice rings out, and Harlow snickers.

"Apologies, ma'am."

Eve narrows her eyes but declares the warm-up over and instructs us to pair up.

"With someone you don't know." She smirks at me.

I end up practicing punching and blocking with a girl named Beth. She's sweet and shy, but her punches feel like a truck as she slams her fist into the pad I'm holding.

"Wow," I say. "Where'd you learn that?"

She blushes. "My mate. He insisted I learn how to throw a punch when everything went down a few months ago with Cheryl."

"Cheryl?"

"Yeah, someone got to her and messed with her meds. She tried to blow us all up." Beth shivers. "Now the Arcav are desperately trying to find out who betrayed them."

Eve blows a whistle, and we switch.

"So," Beth says, huffing out a breath as I jab at the pad. "Are you Jaret's mate?"

"Kind of," I mutter, and just like that, my punch has a lot more force to it.

"Good work, Amanda. Just make sure your thumb is on the outside or you'll break it." Eve nods as I make the change. "Nice."

The mating bands on my wrists are taunting me as I hit the pad, and I wonder if there's a way I can cover them up. Maybe they have something here similar to that thick foundation people use to cover up tattoos.

I'm partnered with Meghan next, who punches and kicks like a whirlwind. I'm gasping for breath as we drop to the ground for push-ups when she broaches the subject of Jaret.

Meghan tilts her head, barely even winded. "You know, I can get you outta here if you want to leave."

I frown. "How?"

"I can fly us out."

"Um. Excuse me?"

"Yeah. Don't give me that look. I'm not just making it up. I've been studying since I got here. Had my first solo flight test last month. Can't say I'd want my first long-haul solo voyage to be all the way back to Earth, but I'm down if you are."

My mouth opens and shuts as I try to find something to say to that. Is this girl for real?

She sighs at the look on my face.

"Here's the thing." She points to her chest with one hand and then resumes her push-ups. "I'm what they like to call a child prodigy. I've got a degree in mechanical engineering, and I'm currently working on my PhD remotely. I was offered a job at NASA but turned it down when Mom found out she was a mate."

"So they've let you learn how to fly here?"

"Yeah. It's been a big learning curve, and obviously I'm nowhere near a pro or anything. But I'm fairly confident I could get us back to Earth without any serious problems." She chews on her lip. "Mom might kill me though."

I burst out laughing. This girl is a total spitfire. "Thanks for the offer. Let's keep that one in our back pocket for now, and I'll try the official way first."

She nods. "Yeah, probably a good plan."

"Ladies!" Eve yells at us from the front of the group. "Can I bring you anything for your chitchat? A cup of tea, perhaps? Maybe a glass of wine?"

I barely resist the urge to flip her off, and she grins at me, a challenge in her eyes.

"God, you guys are crazy," I mutter to Meghan, struggling through another push-up. Mine are knee push-ups, and I'm pleased to see I'm not the only woman gasping for breath.

Meghan laughs. "Yeah. But we're one big crazy family."

CHAPTER SEVENTEEN

Amanda

A week passes. And then a month.

Meghan is moping because Methi disappeared off on some mission without telling her, right after they had a fight. Eve is in a dark mood because she was overlooked for another mission, and Harlow is still puking every chance she gets.

Bree is the only one who seems to be enjoying life. And she truly is thriving. Unfortunately, she managed to convince some poor Arcav to teach her how to drive a pod. As someone who has had the misfortune to drive with her on Earth, there's no way I'm getting in a pod with her and her road rage.

I allow Jaret to come and sit next to me every few days. Harlow explained that even for unmated Arcav who are struggling with their sanity, or those who lost their mates like Korva, simply being around human women helps them regain focus and control.

So we sit, usually in the garden outside my room. He doesn't attempt to speak to me, and I don't say anything to him. I regret telling him I don't want to be his friend. I miss talking to him, learning about him, and simply hearing his voice. But I also know that life can't go back to what it was.

Today, I have my first meeting with Harlow, Varian, and a few of his advisers. I finally feel like I'm making some sort of difference with the work I'm doing, and I love examining Arcav laws to see where they share similarities with human ones. It feels good to look for ways both races can compromise. Realistically, the Arcav hold most of the power in negotiations. They brought a gun to a knife fight, and if they wanted to simply load up every human woman within a certain age range and relocate them to Arcavia, they could probably do it.

But my father was wrong. At their heart, Arcav are just like humans. Some are exceptional, while others are broken. Some are examples of what humans should aspire to be, while others are just plain assholes. One thing they all seem to have in common? Sheer logic. They understand that working with humans will further their goals much more effectively than making us feel like we have nothing to lose. They know it's better to not back us into a corner.

I walk into the meeting room, where some of the advisers are already waiting. Some smile and nod, while others ignore me. When Harlow and Varian arrive, they all jolt to attention.

Harlow makes her way to me. "You ready?"

"Yeah. I'm excited to get started."

Varian takes care of business, listening as various concerns are brought to his attention. Finally, it's my turn.

"I would like to propose a bill that ensures greater sharing of medical knowledge between Arcav and humans."

One of the advisers snorts, and I make a mental note to find out his name.

"You mean Arcav sharing our superior technology and medical knowledge with the humans." The sneer in his voice is loud and clear until Varian lets loose one low growl, reminding everyone at the table that their queen is a human.

I sigh and get to my feet. Time to speak to them in a language they will appreciate.

"Imagine your mate is born on Earth. I guess that's something that is pretty much guaranteed now, right? But what if she's unlucky enough to have a disease like CF? Or cancer? Or any other number of diseases and illnesses that are long gone from Arcavia but kill millions of humans each year? What happens to you when that mate dies as a child or a teenager? While I would love if you decided to begin sharing medical knowledge out of the goodness of your heart, there's no question it will benefit the Arcav too."

Harlow slides me a small smile as I sit back down, and the table is silent.

"Objections?" Varian asks, and none of the Arcav say a word. Harlow has done her research, and she informed me earlier that none of the advisers sitting at this table have found their mates yet.

"In that case, I agree. Zentri, you will work with our healers to find safe ways to share medical knowledge with the humans."

"Does this include the Alni plant, Your Majesty?"

"No. Humans are too fertile to introduce such longevity to their race unless they are mated to Arcav or working in a dangerous role in Arcavia. Their planet could not handle the strain. Is there anything else that must be discussed? I have a meeting with Jaret."

Harlow clears her throat. "Actually, we have one more proposal to discuss."

She gets to her feet, and Varian's eyes follow her every movement.

"It's not fair that women who are mates are automatically forced to leave their lives behind. I know you've made big strides with our previous agreements," she says, shooting him a warm look from beneath her lashes, "but we need more rights, Varian."

He sighs and rubs a hand over his horn as if he already knows he won't like the next words out of Harlow's mouth.

"If human women want to go back to Earth and leave their mates in Arcavia, they should be able to."

The advisers all begin talking over one another before silencing immediately at a glance from Varian, who looks as shocked as I've ever seen him.

"Leave their mates?"

"As we've discussed many times before, a mating doesn't trump free will."

"How do you expect the Arcav to react to this idea?"

Harlow shrugs and shifts slightly, her shirt conforming to the slight mound at her belly. The effect on Varian is instant. His eyes soften, and he looks at his mate as if she is the sun and the moon.

"Maybe it will ensure the Arcav are making their mates happy," she says. "If not, those women should be allowed the choice to return home."

Varian sighs. No one moves an inch as he stares at Harlow.

"I will think on this."

Harlow looks triumphant, her grin blinding.

I lean close to her after most of the advisers have left and while Varian is talking to one of his generals.

"You look pleased."

She nods. "I know it doesn't sound like a win right now. But Varian even considering this type of law is huge. It would be massively unpopular with almost every single Arcav, and he's still thinking about it anyway. That's my man—learning feminism 101."

Harlow blows Varian a kiss as he glances over, and the look he sends her is so heated that I almost blush.

She walks outside with me, and I lower my voice further, conscious the Arcav have much better hearing than us.

"Nice work with the bump shot. Really hit it out of the park."

She bursts out laughing. "You noticed that, huh? Varian feels so bad seeing me throw up all the time, but he's already such a proud papa that I figured I'd nudge him over the line." Her face sobers. "We could have a girl, you know. I want to make sure I'm creating the best possible future for human *and* Arcav women."

"Well, that was impressive."

"So were you. Nice job appealing to the advisers with their future mates." She grins. "Hey, listen, I forgot to tell you, but there's a ball tonight. We have dignitaries visiting from another planet. Varian's hoping to convince other aliens to ally with us against the Grivath. It's gonna be boring, but Eve and Meghan will be there as well, if you and Bree want to come?"

A night out instead of wallowing in bed wondering what Jaret is doing and who he's with?

"Sounds great."

Jaret

I have no desire to be here, talking with dignitaries from Traslann. Right now, they are allied with the Grivath, and I do not want to have them here, on our planet.

Varian is right though—if we can convince them to switch sides, it may just be the leverage we need to take the Grivath down.

One of the reasons the Grivath have been such a thorn in our side is their sheer numbers. They are not particularly smart. They have never surprised us with any great strategy—other than getting their claws on the shielding technology from the Fecax. But they have spread throughout the galaxy, their ships in every corner as they aim to invade every planet and make it theirs.

My uncle appears, and I lift my lip. He knows I do not wish to speak with him, but he enjoys cornering me in public, knowing I do not care to make a scene.

"Hello, *son*," he says, and I stiffen, instantly assaulted by memories of him hissing plans for revenge in my ear night after night.

"What do you want, Iken?"

"Why, merely to say hello. I heard you have mated."

"You heard wrong."

Amanda is here somewhere, a golden flame in a formfitting dress. She no longer talks to me, and every day I wake up mourning the loss of her voice.

"You know, I thought you would have found the Arcav traitor by now. But you are about as good at that as you are at making the Grivath pay for taking your parents. Tell me, does it take work to be this useless?"

I run my eyes over him, and whatever he sees on my face makes him flinch.

"Son—"

"Do not," I say softly, "call me son."

I jerk at a touch on my arm and look down, where Amanda has appeared.

"And who are you?" Iken asks, curling his lip.

She ignores him for a moment, stroking my forearm, voluntarily touching me for the first time in weeks. I look down at her, and I know my eyes are a barren wasteland.

"I'm the woman who knows exactly how you took an innocent, mourning child who just wanted his mama and turned him into a man obsessed with revenge."

Iken's eyes widen. "How dare you!" he hisses.

"No. How dare *you*. I will spend the rest of my life making sure you pay for what you did to that little boy."

"The rest of your short human life? And how do you hope to achieve that?"

"Easy." She turns and waves to Harlow, who winks and waves back. "I've got friends in high places, motherfucker."

The look on Iken's face is priceless, and for the first time in centuries, I want to laugh. Amanda walks away, and I follow her. No one has ever defended me like this. Our relationship has shattered, but this female still gathers up the sharp pieces and attempts to protect me from hurt.

Brexa appears, dressed in a long white gown, a wide smile on her face. It drops when she sees me striding after Amanda and notes the mating bands on her wrists.

"You've mated," she whispers, stopping in front of me while I inwardly curse as Amanda disappears into the crowd.

"I have not," I tell her. "Our agreement still stands."

She smiles bitterly. "And I can see how happy that agreement makes you."

"What do you want from me, Brexa?"

She simply shakes her head. "I have information," she says.

We are in a crowd of people.

"Not here."

I gesture toward the door and follow her out of the ballroom, meeting Varian's eyes on the way.

He nods as he sees where I am going, and I know we will meet soon to discuss any information Brexa has gathered from her maid.

We move close to the window in the hall behind the ballroom, away from prying ears.

"What do you know?"

"Chenda overheard a conversation between a Grivath and a Trasla. She said the Grivath implied they now have spies on every planet they're targeting for invasion. But it's what they're offering that is most interesting."

"What is it?"

She smiles slowly, and her grin widens as my fists clench. I am known for rarely showing any emotion, and I know she believes this reaction is for her. But it is frustration that Brexa is wasting my time when I could be talking to Amanda.

"Kiss me, Jaret," she says. "Kiss me and I'll tell you everything you want to know."

"Tell me first," I grind out, loathing myself.

She bats her lashes at me and then sighs, hopefully beginning to realize I do not find her even a little endearing.

"The Grivath have told the spies they have discovered a small planet on the outer edge of this galaxy. It was previously thought to be incompatible with life, but it appears most beings from the planets the Grivath are targeting will be able to live there. Chenda said the Grivath are promising the spies they can have the entire planet in exchange for betraying their people."

A planet full of spies and traitors. At least now we know what the Grivath are offering. Unlike Varian, I am under no illusions as to the loyalty of citizens on any planet. Anyone can be bought. We need to look for an Arcav who has expressed dissatisfaction in the past. One who would be open to relocating for the chance to be more powerful on a new planet.

"Jaret?"

I frown down at Brexa, realizing she is still there.

"You will kiss me now," she says.

"Brexa—"

"You will kiss me, or I will tell the Trasla that Chenda is spying for us. She will suffer a long and painful death, and you will be no closer to finding your mother's killer."

I reach out a hand and circle her neck. I could snap it with a thought. This female is a snake. One who would see a woman murdered after using her as a spy in order to keep me close. I hold her life in my hands while I consider her fate. If I kill her, I will be put in a cage, unable to get my revenge.

"Brexa," I say softly, leaning closer to her, and she wraps her arms around my neck.

"Yes?" She believes she has won.

I lean even closer, whispering in her ear, "You have proved you cannot be trusted. You may believe you have leashed me with your threats, but you will pay for this."

Her eyes widen and fill with hate as she glances over my shoulder. "Fine. But you will kiss me."

I stare at her, wishing I could wring her neck and feel her last breath as I do so.

And I hear Amanda's shocked gasp as Brexa leans close, her eyes on my lips.

"Jaret?"

CHAPTER EIGHTEEN

Amanda

I'm laughing as we turn the corner, and it turns into a choked cough as I see Jaret. Jaret leaning against the wall. Jaret with his hand out, pressed against the chest of a beautiful Arcav woman.

The woman leans close, and it's only his hand that's stopping their lips from touching.

He glowers down at her, and she smiles, glancing over her shoulder at me. "Your heartbreak is even better than a kiss," she murmurs, glancing at me.

Eve and Bree are silent, although Harlow lets out a small snort and muttered "asshole."

I straighten my spine. I'll fall apart later.

"I wondered how you were so good at that," I say softly. "I guess now I know."

I turn and walk in the opposite direction, not sure where I'm going.

Jaret obviously tries to follow me, because I hear Bree snap at him.

"Leave her alone, you bastard."

My hands shake, and my face burns with humiliation. It's bad enough that Jaret has made it obvious he doesn't want me, but now he's adding insult to injury by publicly making out with someone else?

I laugh humorlessly. The Arcav woman is in love with him. It was written in the torment on her face, and I pity her almost as much as myself. But I would never blackmail a man into being with me.

"Manda? Do you want to talk about it?"

"Later," I choke out. "I just need some fresh air. Alone."

I storm through the halls, making my way to the gardens, which are lit up with tiny lights. The stars shine down, so different from the ones I'm used to seeing on Earth and so much brighter thanks to the clean, clear air in Arcavia.

I jolt as I hear a loud meow.

"What the hell?"

A cat appears out of nowhere and begins winding along my feet. What's a cat doing in Arcavia? I crouch down and let him sniff my hand, reaching for his collar, which has a small silver tag. I let out a wet giggle as I read the inscription.

My name is Tom. I like to wander, and I will hiss at large males. If I'm lost, please return me to Harlow.

"Well, that's adorable. So you hiss at large males, huh? Maybe we can be friends."

I find a bench and sit staring at the garden. I'm surrounded by beauty. I have a cat purring on my lap. I've made friends here. But I'm miserable.

In the nineteenth century, the English were painting arsenic on their walls, fascinated with the emerald-green color. The problem? Those damp English weathers turned the arsenic into gas, sickening and killing those in the room. The greener your walls, the sicker you got.

Now we know it's poison.

Jaret is like that. He's the kind of bright, vibrant color you want to spend time near, cherish, and show off to all your friends. But the longer you stay with a man who is slowly poisoning you, the weaker you get.

"Manda."

I turn. My gorgeous, fun, *alive* sister has come to find me.

"I'm sorry. I couldn't even give you a few minutes. I just wanted to check on you."

I pat the bench beside me, and she sits down, mouth dropping open as she takes in the cat on my lap.

"Wow. How did this happen?" Tom purrs as she scratches beneath his chin.

"He's Harlow's cat." Her mate will do anything to make her happy. The man who should be *my* mate is kissing other women in full view outside public events.

"What are you going to do?"

I shrug. "I don't know. It's killing me, Bree. But I owe him big for what he did for you. And the Arcav can lose their minds if they're away from their mates."

Bree shifts closer. "Okay, first, *I'm* the one who owes him big. Don't you see? You don't always have to sacrifice yourself! I will forever be in awe of your strength and sheer grit getting me here. But you don't have to stay."

"He saved your life, Bree."

"He did. He saved *my* life. And he's ruining yours. You think I don't notice what's happening? I can barely even recognize you anymore! You never talk, you hardly socialize, and you still let him come and sit with you, even while your heart is breaking into a thousand pieces."

"You don't understand."

"When you love, you love with every atom. You deserve to have someone love you back the same way, Manda. If you don't think Jaret can do that, I want you to go and live your life. Take your dream job, but do it in DC. Meet a man who will love you the way you should be loved and make adorable babies for me to cuddle."

She's right. "I do love him. I love him, and it hurts so bad because he'll never choose me over his revenge. But maybe I'm just not destined to live a fairy tale. Love doesn't always mean a happily ever after. Just look at Mom."

"You'll make your own damn fairy tale."

"You know, we're way overdue for a sisterly spat, right?"

Bree grins at me. "Want to steal one of my shirts? Maybe spill something on it?"

I lean my head on her shoulder, sending up a silent prayer to whatever miracle of science brought my sister back.

"I don't want to fight anymore," I whisper. "I'm tired. I want someone who'll fight for me."

One day, Jaret will realize what he's lost. It's a shame I won't be around to see it.

Jaret

I stare at the ComScreen in my hand, barely restraining the urge to smash it into a thousand pieces.

I shove it in my pocket and stalk to my mate's quarters, where I usually meet her around this time. I miss her stories and her gentle teasing.

I did not see her this week, hoping to give her some time after she saw Brexa attempting to kiss me. My hands shake with rage as I remember the look of satisfaction on Brexa's face as she saw the tears sliding down Amanda's cheeks.

I pound on her door, and it opens immediately.

"Oh," Bree says flatly. "It's you."

She is holding a sun hat and purse in her hands, but she turns, and I get my first glimpse of Amanda.

"Do you want me to stay?" Bree asks.

Amanda slowly shakes her head, avoiding my eyes.

Look at me, I want to howl. *Look at me, you traitorous snake.*

Her actions have proved she is no better than Brexa.

"I'll just be in the garden with Eve. Let me know if you need me." With one final glare for me, Bree sweeps out, looking remarkably healthy for a female who knocked on death's door and said hello.

"Look at me," I rasp, and Amanda finally meets my eyes.

I take the communicator out of my pocket. "What were you thinking?"

"What was I thinking? I actually can't believe you're asking me that."

"An application to leave our mating?"

She nods. "You know, I was okay with you taking a little longer to accept the whole mate thing. I was dealing with the sympathetic stares, crying myself to sleep, and even my new jewelry." She holds up one wrist, the black mating band stark against her skin. "But then you publicly humiliated me. It wasn't enough that we can't even speak to each other anymore? You had to twist the knife by getting close to that woman in front of everyone?"

"I have explained the situation with Brexa. She felt threatened and refused to give me some crucial information unless I kissed her. I didn't do it."

"Yeah, you didn't do it because I caught you." She

laughs. "Wow, that's almost as bad as 'I was thinking of you the whole time,'" she mutters.

"She threatened to have the maid spying for us killed!" I roar, barely recognizing myself. I turn and clench my fists, bringing myself under control.

"Oh, look, he does feel," Amanda says sarcastically. "Why would you want to be with someone like that, Jaret? Someone who could threaten an innocent life? Someone who holds you hostage?"

"I have told you," I grind out. "I will not rest until I have destroyed the Grivath. You know what they did to my parents. Can you blame me for wanting them dead?"

"No, I can't. But I would never knowingly allow someone to develop feelings for me if I knew I couldn't return them. And that's exactly what you did, Jaret."

"So this is how you punish me? Threaten to leave?"

Her nostrils flare. "It's not a threat, and it's not punishment. I'm doing what's best for me."

"And what about me?"

"It looks like you're doing just fine to me." Her tone is bitter, and I once again curse Brexa. And then I curse myself.

She sighs. "I understand why you have to spend time with her, Jaret. I get it. You need her for information. But I can't see that every day. I can't deal with how much it hurts. So I'm leaving."

"You will not leave."

"You saved my sister," she says, rubbing a hand over her face tiredly. "And for that, I'll be forever grateful. But now it's time for me to save myself. You're an ice storm, Jaret. And my rainbows can't survive near you."

Amanda

When we're hurt—really hurt—our instinct is to either curl up in a ball and protect ourselves or lash out and hurt the other person just as bad. But when you love that other person, you don't want to hurt them. The thought of seeing them in pain is repulsive. So you have two choices. Stay and be a victim, or leave and be a survivor.

Today is the day Varian will consider my application to leave Arcavia. It's only been three days since I filed the application, and Jaret has thankfully stayed away. I'm pretty sure I have Harlow to thank for this speedy process.

Her proposal is still being considered, and we are all aware that whatever Varian decides today will likely become the precedent for mates in the future.

I think Harlow might be just as nervous as I am. Although, the pained look on her face may just be morning sickness.

I blow out a breath as Jaret walks in, refusing to so much as glance in my direction.

Do I feel like a bitch for doing this? Sure. But the world doesn't stop simply because an Arcav has mated. The strange black markings on my wrists don't have to influence the rest of my life.

At least I hope they don't.

Varian is sitting at the head of the table, and the room is silent. His face is stone, and I can't imagine he is happy he's the one to make this call.

"After carefully reviewing this case, I have made my decision," Varian says, and I blow out a breath, carefully avoiding glancing at Jaret.

"Varian," Jaret begins, but the king simply ignores him.

"I will grant separation rights to Amanda. However, you

will need to return to Arcavia every six months for one week, during which time you will spend five hours of each day in Jaret's company."

All I hear is six months. Six months on my own, without risking my heart each day. Six months without wondering if I'll see him with another woman each time I turn a corner.

"Six months?" Jaret's tone is no longer ice cold. It burns with fury.

Varian gives him a sympathetic look, but his tone is firm. "I am well aware you were in no danger of falling over the edge of sanity before you met your mate. I believe you will be able to continue with your search for the Arcav traitor during this time period. If I believe Amanda needs to return more frequently, we will readjust this schedule." He looks at me, and I nod.

Everyone begins to file out, and I take a moment to let it sink in. It's done. I won. So why don't I feel like celebrating?

I can feel Jaret's eyes on me, and I ignore him.

"Mate," he says softly, and I stiffen at the word, refusing to acknowledge the hurt it causes.

"Amanda," he says, and I finally look up. "Do not do this."

"I'm sorry Jaret, but I have to."

He clenches his jaw. "You were preparing to leave the moment you joined the council. You would never have stayed."

I stiffen. "I joined the council when I still had hope we could be something. I was close to considering Arcavia my new home. You never gave me a reason to stay."

He bares his teeth, showcasing those sharp fangs. I've never once seen them through a smile. "You will never leave me."

I just shake my head. "I loved you, you know. I hope you

find what you're looking for in this life. I want only the best for you."

Jaret stalks out, and I have a feeling he's not going to take this decision well. I've never met anyone who craves control the way he seems to.

I walk directly into Bree's arms. I already decided if I were allowed to leave, I would leave today. No point hanging around and making things more difficult.

"I'm going home," I whisper, and she smiles even as tears fill her eyes.

"I'm so happy for you, Manda."

"Are you sure you don't want to come with me?"

She shakes her head with a grin. We've talked extensively about this. Bree considers Arcavia a fresh start. She's healthy and doing all the things she never got to do on Earth. Honestly, it'll probably do us good to spend some time apart like normal siblings. Even if we do plan to talk twice a day.

Varian appears, and I tense at the look on his face.

"You will not be leaving until later today," he says, his voice a low growl, and Bree trembles beside me. I've mostly seen Varian all loved up and around Harlow, so it can be easy to forget just who he is and how scary he can be.

"Um. Why?"

"Jaret ordered every ship to leave Arcavia or be disabled."

Bree gasps. "That shithead."

"Indeed." He narrows his eyes at me. "I had a feeling he would attempt to stop you, so I made alternate arrangements. That ship will be here in three hours. In the meantime, I must order the arrest of the closest male I have to a friend." He gives me a look that suggests I'm unworthy of such an action, and I struggle not to roll my eyes.

Men. They stick together on every planet.

Bree and I make our way to Harlow and Varian's quarters, where our new friends have gathered to say goodbye. Harlow hands me a glass of wine.

"I heard you'll be here for a few more hours than expected." She gestures to a large table, where heaped plates of both human and Arcav food have been set up.

My heart gives one sad thump as I remember Jaret teaching me the names of some of those foods at Harlow and Varian's wedding. It feels like so long ago, but it's only been a few months.

"Thanks, Harlow. You've been amazing throughout this whole thing."

"I am pretty amazing," she says, winking as she hands Bree a glass of wine. "But you did all the hard work."

I blow out a breath. It's just starting to hit me that I'm actually leaving. I hadn't thought I had a chance, but it turns out Jaret's determination to not complete the mating bond has given me the freedom to make my own decisions.

"Are you going to see him before you go?" Meghan asks just as Eve arrives, handing Harlow another bottle of wine.

"Ooh," Eve says. "Bad idea. What if he works some dick sorcery on her and changes her mind?"

I snort. "I'm not going to change my mind. I would like to say goodbye though."

Bree rolls her eyes. "By that, she means she'd like to apologize profusely as if she's done something wrong."

I elbow her, and she sighs.

"You want me to come with you?"

"I'll think about it."

In the end, I say goodbye to everyone a couple of hours later, hugging them one by one, with promises to keep in touch.

I walk Bree back to our quarters and hand her my element collection. "I'm leaving this with you."

"Oh, Manda. I can't."

"You know why I started collecting them, right?"

"Yeah. So you could play God. It was a little *Pinky and the Brain* of you, but you've always been motivated."

We grin at each other, and tears fill our eyes.

"I don't need them anymore. You keep them here for me, and I'll add to them when I visit."

She nods. "Six months. We can make it that long."

"It'll go by in a blink of an eye."

I don't believe that, of course. My heart is broken, and I'll be completely alone in DC. But I have to try. Maybe being on a different planet will help me find some kind of closure.

We hug, clinging to each other like children. Even though I know this decision is the right one, that doesn't mean it's easy.

Finally, I let her go. "Maybe I'll be able to cut out some of my codependent bullshit if I'm forced to be alone."

Bree rolls her eyes and pulls tissues from her pocket, handing one to me. "You're not codependent. Call me as soon as you arrive."

I nod, turn, and walk away, each step harder than the next. I'm emotionally raw and leaving in twenty minutes, but I can't help myself. I've found out where Jaret is being kept, and I make my way down to the cell underneath the palace.

He's pacing his cage like an animal when I appear and immediately lunges for the bars, snarling at me.

I suddenly realize his eyes aren't cold at all. When he looks at me, his eyes burn like fire.

"Nice try with the ships," I say. "I'm leaving in twenty minutes. I just wanted to say goodbye."

He growls. "You would leave me like this?"

"I'm not enjoying it." I sigh. "Listen. We're not bonded. Varian is right—six months won't be a problem for you. You know you're not risking insanity."

"I never thought you were the type of female to stoop to revenge." His cold voice is like thorns dragging down my skin, and I snap.

"This isn't about revenge, Jaret. News flash, but I don't need to stick around and watch you cozying up to someone else. I would never do that to you. What could possibly make you think that kind of behavior is okay?"

He says nothing, and I laugh bitterly.

"Oh, right. If it's for your precious revenge, it's acceptable."

Our relationship is flickering through my brain like the worst flashback in history. All I can see are closed doors and Jaret's back. Time and time again, he's walked away from me, leaving me wishing he would stay.

This time, I'm walking away from him.

"If you leave me," Jaret grinds out, "I will make you regret it."

I stare at him. Why did I come here? What was I hoping for? An apology? Maybe a change of heart and a declaration of love?

I'm an idiot.

We are ash. The broken powder of burned dreams. But it's not too late for me to find a new dream. I turn, ignoring Jaret's roar as he shakes the bars of his cage.

And I walk out.

CHAPTER NINETEN

Jaret

Varian leaves me in the cage as a warning to anyone who thinks to go against his decrees in the future.

I do not care, and simply lie on the cold floor, contemplating my life. Varian visits on the third day, casting me a look of supreme boredom as he scans his eyes over me.

I tense. "What do you want?"

"Perhaps to let you out."

"Do not bother."

"Ah. This is what Harlow calls a pity party."

My claws extend, and he laughs.

"I have information. We looked into the maid's claim about the new planet. We found it."

I sit up. "Where is it?"

"Close enough to Earth that the humans would be at risk. Of course, if the traitors manage to complete their tasks and win the planet, the Grivath will already have invaded both Earth and Arcavia anyway."

I snort. "Who would be stupid enough to take the word

of a Grivath? They are likely planning to turn it into another slave planet."

"Harlow is currently with the human woman...Cheryl. Meghan is attempting to sketch the face of the traitor based on the woman's limited memories. I need you to retake your place as commander."

He opens my cage and holds out a hand. I ignore it and stand, unwilling to forgive him.

"I made the best possible decision," he says.

"I helped you hunt your mate," I hiss. "You helped mine leave me."

"You chose not to complete the mating bond. I still do not understand why. We both searched for our mates for so long, and then you refused to make your female yours in truth."

I am silent. I do not need to explain my reasoning to Varian. He has everything a male could want.

He frowns at my silence. "What was I to do?"

"Show some loyalty. But I would not expect that of your bloodline."

I shoulder past him, and he stiffens.

"What," he says quietly, "is that supposed to mean?"

I ignore him and keep walking.

"You have let the Grivath take everything from you," Varian says. "Your mother would be so disappointed."

"Your father killed her!" I roar, turning. "Do not presume to tell me what my mother would feel."

His face hardens. "You do not truly believe that."

I ignore him and walk out, making my way to the medi-center, where I find Bree and Meghan with Harlow as she talks to Cheryl. Why must these human females travel in packs?

Meghan wrinkles her nose as I arrive. "Dude," she says,

moving away from me. "You smell like something died, came back to life, and then died again."

I have not yet bathed or changed my clothes, and I merely shrug. Bree glowers at me, and I ignore her, turning to the woman who attempted to assassinate Harlow, Varian, and most of our highest-ranking officials.

"What do you have?"

Cheryl stares at me, quaking, and Harlow frowns.

"Maybe you should go sit in that chair. By the window. Near the fresh air. Until we're done."

I barely refrain from rolling my eyes, a habit I must have picked up from Amanda.

That treacherous witch.

Being near her friends—and especially her sister—is like taking a knife in the gut. I wonder what she is doing now. Perhaps she is finding a human as we speak. One who laughs and shares his *feelings*.

Something cracks, and heads whip toward me. I unfurl my hands from where they have broken the arms of the chair and watch as it repairs itself. The furniture in Arcavia is designed with Arcav strength in mind.

Meghan turns back to Cheryl and raises a sketchbook.

"Where were we?" she asks, and Cheryl gives her a tiny smile.

"His horns were a little longer. And his eyes were closer together. He had a tiny bump in his nose right there."

I frown at the description and turn as I feel eyes on me.

"What?" I growl at Bree, who wrinkles her nose.

"I liked you better when you showered."

I narrow my eyes at her. "I liked you better when you were unconscious."

"That's him," Cheryl says, and Meghan nods, turning the sketchbook around.

"You recognize him?"

My horns straighten, and Bree eyes them warily.

"Yes," I say, my fists clenching as I imagine ripping the Arcav in half. "That is Talis."

Meghan drops the sketchbook, face draining of color.

"You mean the Talis currently on a ship with Methi?"

I nod.

"Oh my God." Harlow's voice is sharp, and she throws an arm around Meghan's shoulder. "Come with me. We'll go find your mom."

Meghan lets her lead her away, and Bree scowls at me.

"Smooth. Way to break the news gently."

I snarl at her, displaying fang, and pick up the sketchbook to show Varian.

Amanda

It's been a month, and life is colorless. There are no rainbows, just gray skies. I did my best to throw myself back into a routine when I returned. I explained my sudden disappearance to my friends, claiming it was a work emergency that required a swift relocation. They didn't exactly buy it. I've been working fourteen-hour days, complete with a packed social calendar in an effort to keep myself busy. Of course, wearing long sleeves in the middle of summer is getting old. I wish I'd asked if there was a better way to cover up these mating bands.

I'm meeting my friend Hayley at a bar in Dupont. She's notoriously late, so I'm finishing up some work, which I'll send to Harlow later.

I thought it would be better if I left. I thought the hole in my heart would mend. But even long workdays and nights out clubbing can't put color back into my world. I've danced on every table in this town, searching for fun...excitement... life. It's nowhere to be found.

"Maybe it'll just take time," Bree said when we video chatted this morning. "A month is nothing, really. Remember when I broke up with Biker Dave and moped for six months?"

I snorted. At least Bree could still make me laugh. Biker Dave had been her attempt to give me a break from my father's constant disapproval. Unfortunately, she caught feelings right around the time he decided he was no longer willing to give up his pack-a-day smoking habit for her health.

"Amanda!"

I stand for a hug, and Hayley steps back, taking a good look at me.

"Jeez, how'd you lose so much weight? Tell me your secrets."

Heartbreak. Lots and lots of heartbreak.

"Gave up sugar. How are you?"

"Oh, you know, same old, same old. Now tell me about this secret project you're working on." She laughs at the look on my face. "I'm kidding. This is DC. If we all started sharing about our secret projects, the city would implode."

Her smile widens as she glances over my shoulder, and I know that smile.

Shit.

Hayley squeals, jumps up, and throws herself into her boyfriend's arms. Of course, her boyfriend, Jason, has brought a friend, who from the look on his face, is also realizing this is a surprise double date. He shuffles his feet, likely preparing for a fast escape, but Hayley grabs his hand, pulling him to our table.

"Corey, this is my good friend Amanda. She just got back from a super-secret trip, and I'm about to torture her for details." She winks at me, and I give her a weak smile, holding out my hand for Corey to shake.

"I know we said a girlie catch-up, but you don't mind if the guys join, do you?"

"Of course not."

Corey is tall and well-built, and his hair has been tousled by the wind. He smells nice, his eyes are blue, and he looks about as enthusiastic about this little surprise date as I am.

This cheers me up, and I grin at him. He smiles back.

"So," Hayley says once our drinks arrive. "Spill all the details about your work trip. You were away for a few months, right?"

"Yeah. It was...unexpected." Might as well lay this out right now and put an end to any ideas about my love life. "I met a guy, and we had a bit of a whirlwind romance. It ended badly, and I'm currently listening to Celine Dion every night until two in the morning," I joke.

Corey relaxes finally, leaning back in his seat. "I just went through a breakup as well. It sucks."

"It sure does."

"Let me know if you want to talk about it sometime. Nothing worse than being surrounded by loved-up couples." He slides a look toward Hayley and Jason, who are feeding each other fries, and I laugh.

"No, I much prefer being surrounded by the cynical and brokenhearted."

"That's the spirit."

I reach for my drink and jerk, knocking it over, as Hayley

reaches out and snags my hand, pulling back my light sweater.

My margarita drips onto the floor as we all stare at the coal-black mating bands.

"Oh yeah," I say, getting to my feet. "The heartbreak? It came from an Arcav. Thanks for the catch-up, Hayley. It's been real."

CHAPTER TWENTY

Jaret

There are many, many ways the Arcav are superior to humans.

But there is perhaps one area where humans excel. Other than the kissing.

Do not think about her lips.

That area is human alcohol.

I take another swig of whiskey, straight from the bottle. I do not know who this Jameson person is, but they have my appreciation.

Perhaps if I drink enough, I will no longer see Amanda's face whenever I close my eyes.

She left me.

She *left* me.

She left *me.*

Varian has visited twice, each time commanding me to return to my duties.

"I gave you my loyalty for close to a century and my trust for longer. In return, you allowed my mate to leave me.

Command your own men," I snarled at him the last time he appeared in my rooms.

He merely looked at me—sprawled on the floor, still wearing the clothes I was arrested in—and shook his head.

"If you are hoping to be the kind of male deserving of a mate, this is not the correct way to do it."

I glowered at him. "You hunted and abducted your mate. She was so desperate to escape that she drugged you."

"Yes. And then I promised to spend the rest of our lives making it up to her."

"GET OUT!"

I lose myself in days of drinking. What is the point of being a male deserving of a mate if she is not here to see it?

I will return to my duties soon. I must continue my quest for vengeance.

So why does the thought of eradicating every last Grivath not bring me the pleasure it used to?

I pass out and dream of Amanda. Her mouth on me, her scent surrounding me. I dream of soft fingers and hot lips. Stiff nipples and long, sleek hair.

"I have missed you, Jaret," she says, and I frown.

"Amanda?"

I open my eyes and roar so loudly that I hear the footsteps of guards running down the hall toward us.

Brexa is leaning over me, her hand sliding down my chest...moving down my body as if she is about to grab my cock.

My hand lashes out, and I grab Brexa by the throat, wanting nothing more than to end her.

"Commander!" a voice yells behind us.

"You *dare* attempt to touch what does not belong to you?"

Brexa gasps, and I let her go. "You are lucky you are a female, or I would kill you."

She gets to her feet, more humiliated at my rejection than hurt from my grip.

"You let her in here without permission?" I ask one of the guards, and he gulps.

"She said she was your woman, Commander. She said she was the reason you sent your mate off planet."

I let out a harsh laugh, and the room goes silent as the guards stare at me in shock. Brexa's eyes widen.

"Never come near me again," I tell her.

She straightens and smiles bitterly. "I think you are forgetting one thing. My intelligence led to the discovery of that new planet," she says. "Are you willing to risk more information that could lead you to the Grivath who killed your parents?"

I narrow my eyes, and it hits me. I have made the worst mistake of my life. I lost the female who made me feel emotions other than rage and hopelessness. And I did it because of my obsession with revenge.

Varian was right. My mother *would* be disappointed. She would be shamed that her son lost the easy smile she loved so much. And she would be furious that I allowed my commitment to finding her killers steal any chance of happiness from me.

"I no longer care."

I nod to the guards, who usher Brexa from my room.

"You will regret this," she hisses.

"I already do," I say, my eyes scanning her cold, furious face.

I feel the intense urge to remove Brexa's scent from my body as soon as she stalks out. I sober up as sweet-smelling steam cleans my body, my Arcav metabolism not allowing me to enjoy the benefits of a good drink for long.

Then I stalk to Varian's quarters, pound on the door, and throw it open.

"I wish for permission to go to Earth."

Varian eyes me from where he stands by the door to his gardens, his hand stroking his mate's hair as she rests her head against his chest. I am so envious that I could tear this room apart.

He obviously sees this on my face, because he sighs.

"Your mate campaigned for the right to live away from you. Why do you believe you should be allowed to follow her?"

"You hunted your mate for weeks, taking her to Arcavia with the use of threats and bargaining."

Harlow opens one eye. "Guy's got a point," she says. "But Amanda made it clear she wants to start a new life. The poor girl has only been home for a month. Why not give her a chance to settle in?"

I think of Harlow's words from the ship when she was taken to Arcavia.

"I hope she hates you," she hissed. "I hope she wants nothing more than to escape you. And I hope she does. Then you'll know what it's like to have everything you value taken from you."

"This is what you wished for," I say. "I hope you are happy."

She frowns at me. "Don't blame me for your shit. The difference between my situation and yours? Amanda *wanted* to stay. She loved Arcavia, and she loved you," she says, and I flinch at the use of past tense. "You're the one who drove her away with your bullshit."

Varian is silent. "I do not believe this is an efficient use of your time," he says. "Your mate has made it clear she does not wish to see you outside of the terms of your mating agreement."

I grit my teeth. I asked the king's permission as a courtesy. I am willing to burn my life down for my female.

Varian stares at me. "Do not do anything stupid," he says softly, and I narrow my eyes at him, disgusted by his hypocrisy.

I glance from him to Harlow, and he sighs.

"Do you think I do not understand the mating urge?"

"I do not care about the mating urge! I care about Amanda."

It's true. I cannot sleep without seeing her face in front of my eyes. Every time I see something I think she would like, I picture her reaction. And then I remember how my actions changed her from a cheerful, passionate female into someone with eyes almost as dead as mine.

Harlow moves away from Varian, stepping toward me.

"I have a suggestion," she says softly, and Varian steps closer to her, embracing her from behind.

"When I was having a hard time accepting my feelings for Varian, I had some sessions with Jen. They really helped."

It takes me a moment to put a name to the face.

"The human talking healer?" My horns straighten in offense. "I do not need to accept my feelings for Amanda. I know what I feel!"

Harlow smiles sadly at me. "Sure. But maybe you need to accept your feelings about yourself."

I glower at her, and Varian steps into my line of vision, his own horns straightening as his claws extend. I take a step back, conscious he is currently even more erratic and protective now that Harlow is carrying his child.

Varian stares me down, and I force myself to take

another step back. I have no desire to make him lose control with his mate in the room. But if he will not be reasonable, I will simply go without his blessing.

"I can have every pilot notified that you are not to board any ship," he says softly, reading my mind. I bare my teeth, ready to make him hurt.

He growls in response and whips out an arm, thrusting Harlow back behind him as she attempts to slip around him to step between us.

"Okay, big guy, threats probably aren't all that helpful right now. Why don't you two make a deal?"

He waits a moment, still glowering at me, and then nods. I barely refrain from snorting at the idea. Harlow and Varian's "deals" are legendary, changing the fate of people on two planets.

Varian narrows his eyes at me. "You will go to my father and ask him about the day your mother died. And you will also go to Jen and talk. If you can convince her your trip to Earth is a good idea, then you may leave."

I nod and turn, immediately creating and discarding plans. One small human female cannot be that difficult to convince, can she?

Jaret

I prowl the room, restless, as the human female—*Jen,* I remember—sits with a serene expression on her face and a cup of Arcav tea in her hand. She has just expressed a fondness for it to me, as if I could care what any human who is not Amanda thinks.

"Why don't you tell me how you're feeling right now?"

I turn, rubbing a hand over my horn in frustration. If only Amanda could see me now. I wonder if she would recognize the male I become without her near.

"I feel resentful that I must waste time here with you when I could be on the way to my mate."

Jen nods. "That's a good start," she says. "Would you like to take a seat?"

I stare at her. I would like to board a ship.

"Let me be clear, Jaret. You will not be leaving Arcavia today or tomorrow. I will not agree to let you leave until I am sure it is in the best interest of both yourself and Amanda."

A snarl rips its way from my chest, the sound brutal. Jen merely raises an eyebrow and makes a note on a tablet in her lap.

"Be aware," she says coolly as she takes a sip of her tea, "that temper tantrums do not inspire much confidence in your mental state."

"What do you want from me?"

"Let's start with honesty. You promise to answer my questions truthfully, and I will advise Varian you may travel to your mate."

"Fine." I slump in the chair and gesture for her to talk.

"Why do you believe Amanda left?"

"Because I refused to open up to her. I treated her coldly."

"Why did you behave that way?"

"I needed her to be close but could not mate with her. I did not want her to have feelings for me when I knew I could never be what she needed."

"Why could you never be what she needed?"

"Because I needed to be with Brexa."

"Truth, Jaret."

My horns straighten in offense. "That is the truth."

"Mmm-hmmm." The human makes another mark on her tablet, and I want to snatch it from her.

"I was with Brexa so I could receive critical information about the Grivath and their plans. I have now admitted to myself I should never have risked my mate for my revenge."

Jen raises her eyes and simply looks at me, lifting her cup to her lips.

I grit my teeth. "I do not know what you want me to tell you."

"Then perhaps you should think about it."

Jaret

After a week of talking with Jen, I am still no closer to leaving Arcavia. Humans and Arcav steer clear of me, well aware of my dangerous mood. I have not forgotten about the second part of my deal with Varian, and I grind my teeth as I knock on his father's door.

"Jaret," Aeton says as he opens it. "Varian said you may want to talk. Please, come in and sit down."

Sonexa walks in, never one to be far from her mate's side. Especially if that mate is having company.

"Why, hello, Jaret. We have not seen you for the longest time."

I shrug, unable to pretend politeness when I am barely holding myself together. Varian has indeed made it clear I am to stay on planet. I was refused entrance to the dock today, with three of my men quaking as they were forced to give me the news.

"Take a seat," Sonexa says when I do not respond.

I nod and sit in an armchair. Sonexa has an obsession

with redecorating, and these quarters are continually changing. Now the walls are a pale blue, reminding me of the human medi-center where Bree lingered so close to death.

I stare at Aeton, so strong and vital and alive. "I want you to tell me about my mother's death."

He spreads his hands wide, leaning back in his chair. "I imagined we would have this conversation decades ago. What would you like to know?"

"Everything."

He nods. "Most people know your father and I were close. But before he met your mother, it was your mother and I who were best friends."

He smiles at the look on my face.

"For a brief period of time, we wondered if perhaps we would be mates in the future. But it was simply a deep friendship. And then Syri met your father, and from that moment, her heart beat for him." He sighs. "Thorde was a good male, but he could be jealous. Syri knew this and had a tendency to indulge him. As we all do with those we care about." He turns his eyes to Sonexa, and we both watch as she pretends to ignore him, her horns straightening dangerously.

"Although we were not as close as adults, being that we were mated to others, we knew each other."

His voice breaks, and Sonexa comes closer, stroking a hand along the back of his neck. It is well known their mating is not a happy one, yet she still is compelled to give him comfort.

The way I should have comforted Amanda.

"I watched as they tortured her, opening her up just to see her bleed, and I saw the look in her eyes. It was the most difficult decision of my life and one that still haunts me in my dreams. If I had allowed the Grivath to land on Arcavia, where the biggest piece of her heart lived"—he inclines his head toward me—"your mother would have gutted me herself. She gave me one small nod, and even smiled at me, as I made the call."

"She should not have been in that position!"

"Syri knew what would happen if she were caught on the mission, and she accepted it. To say anything else is to steal that decision from her."

We sit in silence for a moment.

"And my father?"

"After years of friendship, we were as close as brothers. When Thorde watched his mate die, he swore I had made it happen out of jealousy. He declared I was in love with your mother and had decided if I could not have her, nobody else would. I gave him time. Truthfully, I could barely function myself in the days following your mother's death."

Aeton closes his eyes. "I was planning to visit him, but he took his own life before I could."

"Thank you for your time," I say, standing as Aeton's eyes shoot open in surprise. I go directly to Jen's quarters.

I expect her to ask me about my talk with Aeton. Varian has likely told her our meeting was part of his deal. But she surprises me with a different question.

"You met Amanda's father. What did you think of him?"

"He was a terrible father. From her stories, he sounds cold, unloving, and manipulative."

She nods. "It's likely Amanda would be wary of seeing those qualities in a man again, wouldn't she?"

It takes me a moment. "I am nothing like her father!"

Then I think about it.

From the moment I met Amanda, when I left her alone in a cage with the dead Grivath who attacked her, I have treated her as a convenience, to engage with solely at my pleasure. I have never given her sweet words, or even any indication I felt more for her than simply lust. I almost kissed another female in front of her, even though the thought made my skin crawl. I have pushed her away over and over again, likely the same way she witnessed her father push away her mother.

Would I have done that to her? Beaten her down over the centuries?

Centuries.

I jolt to my feet, every muscle trembling.

"She never had the Alni plant," I growl. "We discussed it, but she never committed to the decision before she went back to Earth. She could die any day. Today, tomorrow. She could be dead now."

"Jaret. I assure you she's not dead."

"How do you know?"

"She talks to Bree in the morning and evening."

"It has likely been at least five hours since Amanda has spoken to her. How do you know she is not dead?"

I pace, imagining my mate, lying somewhere, dying slowly while I talk about my *feelings.*

Jen shrugs, and I want to kill her for that dismissive movement.

"The chances are so low that they are not worth thinking about. If humans took every action wondering if it might kill them, we'd never get anything done."

CHAPTER TWENTY-ONE

Jaret

A week later, I stalk into the human talking healer's quarters, finding her eating lunch with her daughter. Meghan has dark circles under her eyes and is absent any witty remarks. She simply nods at me, gathers her lunch, and walks out the door.

Every minute is excruciating, and I have begun begging Bree each day for news of Amanda. She usually sighs, informs me she is still alive, and closes the door in my face.

Jen frowns at me. "I was enjoying eating with my daughter."

I sit in my usual seat. "I would enjoy eating my mate's cunt."

Her mouth drops open, and I raise a brow as a snort of laughter escapes her.

"I wonder if your mate will even recognize you."

I freeze. "Really?"

She holds up a hand. "That's not a bad thing, Jaret. You're finally allowing yourself to feel and respond to those feelings. You may need to get the hang of responding appropriately, but at least you're starting somewhere."

I simply nod. I know now that I cannot blame my longing for Amanda on our lack of mating.

It wasn't being without my mate that made me quick to rage. It was being without *Amanda*.

"I understand now," I tell her.

"Oh?"

I get back up and pace, unused to this feeling of vulnerability, of helplessness. The last time I felt this way was after my parents died.

"I was allowing Brexa to play her games because I was afraid to be with Amanda." I glare at her. "And if you tell anyone I said that, I will make you pay," I snap.

She writes something on her tablet. "Threats are noted," she says, "and as I've already mentioned, these sessions are completely confidential."

I slump back on the sofa, and it responds accordingly, shifting to accommodate my body. My thoughts immediately return to Amanda, and I almost smile as I remember her reaction to Arcav furniture each time she encountered it.

"Jaret?"

"Yes?"

"Why were you afraid?"

I bury my face in my hands. "Amanda is...fierce. She fights for everyone. She would have fought for me if I had allowed her to. She feels *everything*. And she is *good*. She could have demanded I destroy her father for the way he treated her. But instead, she simply moved on with her life, focusing on the *good* parts." I raise my head. "I am not enough for a female like her. I do not deserve to be with her."

In this moment, I loathe myself for losing the best thing that ever happened to me. My defining moment wasn't the moment my mother died. It was the moment I saw Amanda staring back at me from inside that cage, so scared yet defiant.

Jen gives me a tiny smile.

"You've done some great work, Jaret. Now let's talk about *why* you believe you are not good enough."

I instantly open my mouth, a refusal on the tip of my tongue, and then I snap it shut. If this is what it takes to get to my mate, I will lay all my darkest secrets and weakest emotions at this female's feet.

I open my mouth again, and this time I tell her everything.

Amanda

Summer has become fall. This is Bree's favorite time of the year in DC. Me? I love the spring. This year, however, I'm able to see the bright side that comes with cooler temperatures. I can wear all the sweaters I need to and pretend my dark mating bands don't exist.

I've struck up an unlikely friendship with Corey. It's nothing romantic. Just two lonely people dealing with our failed relationships while everyone around us seems to be in love.

"You're doing it again."

I sigh. I can't stop looking at the place where his horns should be.

"Sorry."

Corey runs a hand through his hair. "Hey, I get it."

We're walking toward my apartment. Turns out Corey lives on the next street, and he's also the perfect gentleman, walking me home on his way after we grabbed a late coffee.

Corey is still in love with his ex-fiancée, who slept with his best friend a week before they were supposed to get married.

I, on the other hand, am attempting to get over a love that was truly out of this world.

I snort.

Corey pinches me, and I yelp.

"You're doing it again," he says, and I groan.

"Do you think it'll ever get better?"

"Hey, don't ask me. I'm still listening to Celine Dion," he says, and we both burst out laughing.

And then I choke on my laugh and we both freeze as a seven-foot man with horns steps into our path.

"Jaret?"

"Wow, this is him, huh?" Corey gulps, and I ignore him, my eyes drinking in the sight of Jaret's face. "You need me to try and fight him?" Corey asks, and Jaret's eyes narrow.

"I'm good."

"In that case, I'm outta here."

"Your lover is a coward," Jaret says as we watch Corey hurry away, and just like that, my rose-colored glasses fall off.

"He's not my lover. What the hell are you doing here?" I ask, thankful it's dark. "You're going to start a riot."

Humans know where we stand on the food chain when it comes to the Arcav. But between the Arcs—Arcav groupies—and the HAA members, Jaret shouldn't have come alone.

I shake my head firmly. He shouldn't have come at all.

"I need to talk to you."

"Jaret—"

"Please. Just five minutes of your time."

"Well," I mutter as I swipe my key fob for my apartment building. "That's the first time I've ever heard you say please, so it must be important."

I'm stunned into silence as we get into the elevator, and I watch him out the corner of my eye as he hunches his shoulders while his horns brush the ceiling. I don't know what he's doing here, but I'm gradually rebuilding the stone wall around my heart as we ascend to my apartment.

I unlock the door and watch as Jaret takes a deep breath. I instinctively know he's seeing if he can scent another man, and I roll my eyes.

"What are you doing here?"

"Can we sit down?"

I sigh but nod, leading him into my small living room. My sofa doesn't adjust to his body, and I smile sadly as I remember my excitement when I first tried Arcav furniture on his ship. It feels like it was so long ago.

Jaret meets my eyes, and I know he's remembering the same thing. He reaches for my hand, and I hesitate until he suddenly pulls me onto his lap.

"Hey!"

"I have come a long way, mate. It is only fair you sit close to me."

I laugh—a cold laugh that doesn't sound like me. A laugh I learned from spending time around the ice man himself.

"I'm not your mate," I say, holding out my wrist. "I'm currently looking for someone who can cover these up. Any recommendations?"

He nods. "I deserve your anger."

Somehow, his acceptance of my bitchiness just makes

me feel worse, and I push against his chest, furious when he refuses to let me go.

"You said I could have five minutes."

I fold my arms like a bratty child, hating, *hating* that my lip trembles. Why did he have to come here? I was doing so well.

Sure, if you call losing twenty pounds and self-medicating with alcohol and Celine doing well.

Jaret blows out a breath, and I take a moment to study him, pushing my hurt to the side. He seems...nervous. His eyes are clear and somber, but I don't feel like I'm looking at a corpse when I look into them anymore. He's studying every inch of my face as if he can't quite believe he's near me, and I sigh, gesturing for him to talk.

He gets straight to the point.

"My uncle beat me every day of my life until I was strong enough to fight back. He told me I was worthless, stupid, and good for only one thing—avenging my parents' deaths. This kind of behavior is...exceptionally rare amongst our people. I knew if I told anyone what he was doing, it was unlikely they would believe me."

A tear slips down my cheek, and Jaret catches it on one finger, bringing it to his lips.

"I was a bad seed, you see. My parents were dead, and I began acting out, fighting with whoever I could. It didn't take much for Iken to paint me as a problem, a liar, and even a thief."

My heart is aching. "Jaret—"

He just shakes his head. "He told me I was responsible for my mother's death. That if I had been a better son, she would have wanted to be home with her family and not fighting the Grivath. He took everything I loved away from me. I could not risk showing any sign of interest in anything, because it would immediately disappear. I became hard, cold, and used to losing the things—and the people—I loved."

"I'm going to kill him."

Jaret brushes my hair back from my face. "From the moment I saw you in that cage, I wanted you to be mine. You were so furiously, vibrantly alive, and I had not realized how numb I had become. Yes, I wanted revenge. But I also did not believe I could be enough for a female like you."

"How could you think that?"

"I have pushed everyone away in my life, including my mate. How could I not think that?"

More tears spill, and he leans closer, kissing each one off my cheeks.

"I am broken," he says, touching a finger to my trembling lips. "Broken but mending. And I will work until I am whole enough to be a male you can be proud of. I love you, Amanda. I would endure every second of my childhood, every lonely moment to find you."

I bury my face in his chest, sobbing. "I've missed you so much."

He lets me cry it out and then gently pushes my head back so he can wipe my tears. I reach up and pull him close, finding his lips with mine. It's unlike any kiss we shared before—this time soft and gentle and sweet. I open my mouth, and his tongue caresses mine.

I feel him hard and ready beneath me, and I shiver in anticipation.

Jaret growls at the movement and stands with me in his arms, laying me back on the couch. He deepens the kiss, and I cling to him, desperate for this man who has traveled across worlds to find me.

He pulls off my sweater, and we both stare at the bands

on my wrist. He takes a moment to gently kiss each one, and more tears fall from my eyes at his tenderness. Then he peels off my shirt and snaps open my jeans, dragging his teeth and lips down my neck.

I feel light-headed with pleasure and happiness, and Jaret pauses suddenly, moving back a few inches and simply looking down at my body.

And then he smiles, and my heart stops at the sight. It's the first real smile I've ever seen on his face, and it's so open and sweet—and damn him, sexy—that I almost pinch myself to check if I'm having yet another dream.

He rips off my bra with one claw and lowers his mouth to my breast, where he flicks at my nipple. I arch into his mouth, groaning, and wind my fingers into his hair, feeling him tense as I brush his horns.

I grin, caressing them again. "Sensitive?"

Jaret lets out a low laugh and peels off my jeans. And then his mouth crashes into mine, and I realize he somehow got naked as I bask in the feel of his warm skin against my own. He grips my thighs and pulls me to the edge of the sofa, dropping to his knees.

I tense, writhing at the first lick of his tongue against me.

"Jaret, please." I grab his horns and almost come from the sight of him between my legs, eyes glowing in pleasure, a slight smile on his face.

"Inside me," I order, and he frowns like I'm ruining his fun. "Later," I say. "I need you inside me."

He leans over me, taking my mouth, and then runs the edge of one claw down my body.

"Mine," he snarls, and then he's nudging at my entrance, a groan escaping us both as he thrusts inside. He stills, allowing me to adjust to his size, and then begins a slow rocking that drives me crazy.

"Jaret—"

"Tell me."

I know what he wants to hear. "I love you."

He moves deeper inside me, and I gasp. "I love you," I repeat and curse as he alternates slow thrusts with pounding movements, driving me crazy with want.

"You're mine too," I whisper, and then I'm crying out as release tears through me, and I'm coming harder than I've ever come before, and my wrists ache for a moment, and then I feel *everything*.

Jaret roars as he comes, and I smile up at him as I feel every ounce of his pleasure deep inside.

His eyes meet mine as we both pant, and he grins as he takes one of my wrists in his hand—such a different reaction to the last time we were in this position.

He seems to read my mind, because he leans over and kisses me gently, and I can feel the deep guilt that tears through him.

"I have treated you so badly. And I do not deserve you. But I am asking you to give me another chance to be the mate you deserve. I know I am not what most females would want for a mate, but every part of my cold heart belongs to you. Please, Amanda. Please come back to Arcavia with me."

He kisses the silver bands, which glow like the prettiest jewelry. "I am sorry if I made you believe even for a second that you were unworthy to be my mate. It was I who was unworthy of you."

"You weren't unworthy, Jaret. You were just suffering. I want to come back with you. I do. But I'm not ready yet."

He closes his eyes, and I can feel his despair.

"Hey," I say, cupping his cheek until he opens his eyes

again. "This isn't a punishment. You hurt me, and I need to feel safe with you before I return to Arcavia."

He nods, his jaw tightening as his eyes flare with determination. "I understand. I will make sure you feel safe with me, Amanda."

I grin. "I know you will. Let me show you my city, Jaret. Let's just enjoy each other."

He smiles crookedly, and my heart melts. I can't wait to have fun with him.

"I love you," I say again, and I'll repeat it as often as I need to until this proud, broken man feels worthy.

He slowly begins to slide out of me, and I moan.

"So," I gasp. "What took you so long?"

EPILOGUE

A manda

Two months later...

I stretch, smiling as I take in the large man sleeping beside me. He has gone back to sleep after our early morning activities, and I blush as I recall just how he made me squirm.

Jaret in the morning...when I have him all to myself...

There are no words for his lazy, wicked touch and the heated look in his glazed eyes.

Jaret is grumpy and occasionally cold, and he sure as hell doesn't play well with others.

But he plays well with me.

I've slid back into life in Arcavia as if I never left.

We spent a month on Earth. Longer than I'd imagined, but apparently Jaret had spoken to Varian about taking some time off. Jaret had brought a few guards with him, so I didn't need to worry about him being vulnerable while we were out exploring DC. We went to shows, wandered through museums, got frisky in the dark at the movie theater, and took long walks. We had picnics in the park and breakfast in bed and barely took our hands off each other the whole time.

Our return trip felt a lot like a honeymoon, and Jaret and I spent most of the time locked away in his quarters.

I feel like I'm walking on a cloud. Like it should be illegal to be this happy.

Even with everything that has been going on with the Grivath, I still have a deep sense of contentment I've never felt before.

I hang out with Bree regularly, but we've graduated from a *need* to be close to simply enjoying each other. Without her CF casting a constant shadow, we can simply be sisters. She's active and social but occasionally falls into bouts of depression. She says it's survivor's guilt. She gets to live a healthy, normal life, but her friends with CF aren't so lucky.

Five of the human women sold by the Grivath have been found and returned home. Varian has sent more Arcav to track the rest of them down, vowing he will discover who they were sold to and where they're being kept.

Meghan and I have grown close, but the excitable, enthusiastic girl I first met is nowhere to be found. She argued with Methi before he left, and his ship has now been missing for ten weeks.

"We were best friends," she told me. "And then we, you know."

I raised an eyebrow. "Ah."

"No—I mean we made out. And he acted like he'd poured kerosene on me and lit the match. You should've seen the look on his face, Amanda. So we fought. And he left. And now he could be dead or dying, and it's all my fault."

She's doing everything she can to find where his ship could be and currently driving Varian crazy with her theories.

Jaret opens his eyes, and I smile as he catches me staring at him. I've become *that* woman. The one who watches her man sleep.

His eyes still have a self-satisfied gleam in them from when he watched me move above him earlier, and I can't help but laugh as we grin at each other like two children up to no good.

His communicator sounds an alert, and he reaches for it, instantly tense.

"What's wrong?"

Jaret takes a moment to read, his golden skin paling as he rubs a hand over his face.

"Varian has installed another spy in Traslann, and they found no trace of Chenda—Brexa's maid. According to the new spy, Chenda hasn't been there for three years. Varian believes Brexa had her killed and has been feeding me scraps of information that she knew herself."

He turns, reaching for me, and wraps me in his arms. "She knew that information because she was also betraying our race."

"Oh, Jaret."

"I trusted someone who colluded with my mother's murderers. Someone involved with slaughtering the Fecax royal family and leaving the princess orphaned and alone. If she is even alive."

"You haven't heard from Roax?"

He shakes his head. "He cannot locate her."

I want to make Brexa pay. "Where is Brexa now?"

"She has disappeared, likely aware Varian was close to discovering her treachery. I...do not understand. First Talis and now Brexa. How many more traitors and spies will we discover? How deep does this go?"

"I'm so sorry, Jaret."

He sighs, nuzzles into me, and whispers in my ear, "Are you ready for your surprise?"

I raise an eyebrow at the abrupt change of subject. "Don't you want to talk about this some more?"

"Not now. I will no longer focus on the Grivath to the exclusion of my mate. I promised to take you somewhere special. Are you ready?"

I glance down at my very naked body. "Um..."

He merely grins, and I grin back. I never get tired of seeing his smile. Then he pulls the covers off me and hauls me to my feet, wrapping me in the bright-pink sundress he peeled off me last night.

"Jaret!"

"Just...trust me."

He contacts someone on his communicator while I brush my teeth, and as soon as we step out into the garden, a pod arrives.

"Where are we going?"

He simply narrows his eyes at me, and I smirk as I take my seat in the pod. Worth a try.

We fly away from the palace, toward a less populated area of the city, and I gasp as a gorgeous house comes into view, wrapped in a wild garden. I jump out of the pod the moment we land, my feet itching to explore. I'm turning toward a small stream when Jaret grabs my hand, pulling me toward the house.

Although, the word *house* doesn't seem grand enough for this incredible property. It's huge, with a wide porch and the glass walls the Arcav prefer. But it's also homey, with a few pieces of furniture that seem reminiscent of what I'd see on Earth. I wander the house, Jaret silent beside me, although I can feel his eyes on me.

"What is this place?"

"My childhood home. I have both good and bad memories here. Before my parents died, it was everything I could have wanted a home to be. Then my uncle moved in, and it became a living hell." He shrugs. "In spite of that, I feel compelled to visit this place every so often. I would…like to make some new memories here. With you."

I turn to him, encouraging him to bend down so I can take his face in my hands.

"I love this place. I'd love nothing more than to fill it with happy memories."

I feel like my face might crack under the weight of my grin. Neither of us had what you'd call a normal childhood. Both of us are still healing. But we'll create our own home here.

"Do you love me?" I would think Jaret is joking, except I can hear the vulnerability in his voice and the mating bands allow me to feel the tiny spark of fear I might one day say no.

"Of course I love you."

He takes my mouth, and I sigh into his kiss.

Jaret growls, and I grin into his mouth, chest tight with happiness. I traveled into space, and in the center of it, I found a gravitational force I couldn't escape. His name is Jaret, and everyone thinks he's cold and remote. But I see the real him. And he's beautiful.

The End

Thanks for reading the Arcav Commander's Human. If you enjoyed this book, please consider leaving a review :)

Want to be the first to know about new books, cover reveals, audiobooks and sales? Sign up for my free newsletter at hopehartauthor.com

I'm also active on Facebook. Come say hi at Hope Hart Author.

Keep reading for a sneak peek of the first chapter of the next book in this series: The Arcav General's Woman.

THE ARCAV GENERAL'S WOMAN

Methi

The ship shudders around me and I wake, pulled from dreams of *her*. It feels as if we are landing, but that cannot be right.

Talis and I were sent on this mission by Varian, our King. The goal is to stabilize Fecax after the planet's princess was kidnapped and the royal family was slaughtered. With the Grivath invading and enslaving planets across the galaxy, the Fecax rely on our alliance.

But Fecax is still days away.

I reach for my weapon, rubbing one of my horns as I slowly awaken. We are not due to land for at least three more cycles. Has Talis changed the plan? He has been acting increasingly erratic. Small changes, as if his reactions are off. Perhaps he is feeling the need to mate. My jaw clenches at the thought.

The lights are low, and I trip over something solid as I

leave my quarters, almost falling to my knees. I lean down and my hand brushes hair and cold flesh. One of the crew.

My heart thumps harder in my chest and my horns straighten at the threat. Have we been boarded? How did I not wake? I sprint toward the control center, finding more dead crew members on the way.

I open my mouth to call for Talis and then snap it shut. If enemies have boarded our ship, I must practice stealth. My mind returns to dark hair, bright blue eyes, and a quick grin, and something like regret makes my chest ache.

Concentrate.

The ship is a graveyard. Why did Talis not send up an alarm? How did my men die without my knowledge?

I move closer to the control center and freeze as I hear voices. Is that... Talis? I open my mouth to call to him. Is he unaware of the danger? I freeze as a feminine voice sounds. We have no females on this ship.

"I had to leave. I could not take it one moment longer."

Brexa? Varian's cousin? Why is she talking to him on the ComScreen while we are under attack? I cannot be awake. Surely, this is just a nightmare.

Talis's voice is hard. "Why would you leave your post? I believed we had an agreement."

I slam my mouth shut as bile creeps up my throat. No. Not Talis. He is a trusted Arcav general.

"He left me, Talis. He left me for *her*." Rage has filled Brexa's voice.

Talis sighs. "I know, my love. He will pay. They will all pay."

"Varian discovered that Chenda is dead."

A long silence.

"I thought that you had it handled. We have been using her to pass false intel to Jaret for years."

"So did I! How was I to know that the Trasla would finally agree to negotiate with Varian?"

Traitors. Both of them. The Trasla have been allied with the Grivath for centuries, and Varian has been attempting to sway them to our side for just as long.

My hands fist, blood dripping from my knuckles as my claws cut into my palms.

Brexa may only be present via a ComScreen, but I will make her watch as I kill Talis for his treachery.

I stalk toward Talis, weapon in my hand. Brexa calls out a warning, and I jolt in pain as something hits me from behind. Everything goes black.

Meghan

The medi-center is interesting. Of course, everything on this ship is interesting. We've just been attacked by Grivath- a real-life space battle, and my adrenaline is pumping.

Of course, I was unlucky enough to get knocked out, spending most of the battle unconscious.

Typical.

I follow Harlow into a private room. She wants to check on one of the generals who was injured. I like that about her— that she actually cares and doesn't just put on a show like most adults.

Apparently, this Methi guy saved her life and lost an arm in the process. If not for him and the other brave Arcav, the Grivath might have made their way back to where the unarmed humans were hiding.

I freeze as I run my eyes over the man in the bed. His arm is in a weird glass machine that pumps out gas every so often. I hate it. The thought of this strong, brave guy losing an arm hurts something inside me.

The healer explains that the machine will keep his arm in stasis until it can be replaced.

And then Methi opens his eyes.

They're beautiful, like the rest of him, a light blue, almost violet. Those eyes meet mine, and I have the weirdest feeling like I've known him all my life.

There you are.

My gaze goes lower, and I want to lick my lips.

"Methi," Harlow says, ice in her voice. "She's sixteen."

He removes his gaze from me, and I mourn the loss as he frowns in confusion. I do the same. What does my age have to do with anything?

"She's a child," Harlow says, and my mouth drops open as I choke on my spit.

"I'm almost seventeen," I say, blinking back tears. Teenage hormones are the worst. "And that was mean, Harlow."

I leave before I can do something even more embarrassing, like burst into tears.

I lay my head on my arms, my gaze on the garden. Outside, Harlow's cat stalks through the bushes. A few months ago, something mauled that cat, and Varian tried to keep it from Harlow, taking Tom to the medi-center to be fixed before she found out about it.

Unfortunately, Harlow ended up in that medi-center and found her cat, right before she learned that she was pregnant.

Harlow told me that Varian promised not to keep something like that from her again. Sounds nice in theory, but I think these guys can't help but be overprotective.

I frown in thought. Is it nature or nurture? What makes the Arcav so different from humans in so many ways, yet so similar in others? My mind immediately begins spinning. I wonder how many genes the Arcav have. I'm more interested in the Arcav machines than the people, but *everything* in Arcavia is interesting.

"Meghan?"

I turn as my mom walks in. We've got pretty good digs in Arcavia. We had the option of moving out and living near most of the other humans, but Harlow said that there was more than enough room in the palace and hooked us up with an awesome apartment. It even has a small office for my mom to see patients.

Mom's a therapist. Yeah, I know, fun, right?

We're pretty close though. I'm an only child, which could've made me a weirdo, especially when you consider my IQ. But mom did everything she could to make sure I was as well-adjusted as I could be.

"What's up?" I ask.

Mom smiles sympathetically and I almost roll my eyes. I'm so sick of people giving me pitying looks. Methi's *not* dead. He's going to come back, and I'll be saying a big fat *I told you so* to anyone who gave me that look.

"Arax and I are going to go to the market. Do you want to come do some shopping? Maybe grab dinner?"

Arax is my new alien stepdad. Sounds weird, but he's a good guy. He worships the ground my mom walks on, and he's the reason we got to ditch Earth for a way cooler planet.

When the Arcav invaded, they could've demanded anything. The firepower on their spaceships could've made Earth burn. But at first, all they wanted was for every woman on Earth to do a simple blood test. That blood test would determine if they were compatible as mates. Once they were mates, they were shit out of luck. They had to give up their careers, and their lives, moving to Arcavia with their new mates. Thanks to Harlow, it's not as bad anymore. Women who already have husbands and kids don't have to leave if they don't want to. Oh, and Harlow also managed to put an end to blood tests on anyone under eighteen.

Harlow is a total boss.

When I found out that mom was a mate, I insisted that we come to Arcavia right way. A chance to see a new planet, learn about Arcav technology, and escape Earth? I was all in.

"No thanks."

Mom clears her throat.

"Honey..."

"I don't want to talk about it."

Here's what you should know: Before Methi broke my heart, he was my best friend. I haven't had a lot of friends in my life. Being that weird kid who was in high school when kids my age were still learning to read probably had something to do with it.

But Methi somehow got it. He got *me*. And he *liked* that I was weird, and smart, and questioned everything. We'd spend hours together while he talked to me about Arcavia and introduced me to his world.

I'm annoyed at everyone. I'm fighting with my mom, mad at Arax, and Jaret's still not convinced that I should be allowed to train with the Arcav. I've snuck off to my secret spot, a small lake hidden in the forest behind the palace.

Bushes rustle and I spin, annoyed that my hiding place has been discovered. My mouth drops open as I meet Methi's eyes.

"How'd you know I was here?"

He grins at me. "Where you go, I go."

. . .

A few weeks ago, we found out that Methi was on a ship with Talis, the Arcav traitor. They'd left on a trip to Fecax—home to allies of the Arcav. The royal family had just been slaughtered- all but one of the young princesses who'd already gone missing weeks before. Varian says that Talis wouldn't have expected the Arcav to discover he was working for the Grivath and was likely planning to continue the trip to Fecax as planned.

Varian was ready to surprise Talis with an arrest when they landed in Fecax, but last night, the ship veered off course and went completely dark. Talis must've realized Varian was onto him and disabled the tracking sensors.

I'm not an idiot. I know things aren't looking good for Methi. But he's smart. He's a survivor. And he's *not* dead. He'll get through this and come out swinging.

Mom sighs but leaves. Technically, I could have my own place in Arcavia. But I know mom likes having me around, and it's nice to hang out with her.

When she's not psychoanalyzing me, that is.

Methi is my closest friend here. Sure, I hang out with Harlow, Eve, and now Bree and Amanda. But my friendship with Methi is special. At least it was until he suddenly left me with no warning.

That's what men do, Meghan.

I bury that thought. It doesn't matter. Methi was the one I clung to when I first arrived here. The one who hooked me up with a chance to learn how to fly honest-to-god spaceships. And he was all I could think about when I took my first solo flight a few weeks ago.

I get to my feet. Enough moping around. I need to convince Varian to let me look at the information about

Methi's flight path. Maybe I can help figure out where they were headed.

I mosey down to Harlow and Varian's quarters. They're pretty chill considering they're royalty. You don't have to make an appointment to see them or anything. At least I don't, 'cause I'm friends with Harlow. Varian tolerates my spontaneous visits because it makes Harlow happy. I swear that guy would do anything to see her smile.

I greet the guards outside their door and knock twice, almost vibrating with impatience.

"Enter," Varian's deep voice sounds, and I throw open the door, finding Harlow in her usual spot, sipping tea on the gel sofa.

Her pregnancy has been tough, and she generally walks around looking pale and sweaty, as if constantly on the verge of tossing her cookies. I don't know why you'd want to play host to something that's gonna tear open your hoo-ha and then boss you around while stealing your sleep but to each their own.

"Meghan! I haven't seen you in a while. How are you doing?"

There it is, that sympathetic smile.

"I'm fine. How are you? How's the bump?"

I nod toward her stomach, where she's barely showing.

"I'm pretty sure I felt a kick last night. It's still too soon for Varian to feel much, but it made up for some of the puking."

I grin and slump beside her on the couch.

Varian's sitting by the window, working on his communicator and I nod toward him.

"Is he busy?"

Harlow frowns, her concerned gaze turning to Varian.

"Yeah. He's barely sleeping while he tries to find the new

Fecax Queen, smoke out the other traitors, and locate Methi's ship."

"That's actually what I wanted to talk to you guys about."

Harlow shifts, her gaze landing on my face. Talking to her is sometimes as bad as talking to my mom. She's an ex-cop, which means she sometimes gets this steely look in her eyes that warns you to be straight with her. I plan to master that look one day.

"I want access to everything available about Methi's ship and flight path."

Harlow nods slowly, like she was expecting this exact request. "Why do you think you'll be able to find something that the Arcav haven't found?"

She's not being snarky, she's just weighing up pros and cons.

"My supercharged IQ, of course." I send her a shit-eating grin and she smiles back.

The polite term is *gifted*. The more common term is *freak*. I'm the girl who ruined the curve for people ten years my senior. It's not my fault I was a child prodigy. When I was younger, I would've given anything to be normal. Now, I own my genius— for the most part. If I can use it to help find Methi, then maybe all the years of being a freak will be worth it.

"You know, the Arcav are pretty intelligent."

I send her a look. "Of course they are. But how much can it hurt to get another pair of super-smart eyes on it? Maybe I'll spot something they've missed."

She looks at me for a moment longer and then nods her head. Harlow loves Methi like a brother. She'll do anything to help find him.

Harlow turns to Varian, who's already walking toward us. He stands behind the sofa and strokes a hand down the back of Harlow's hair as he narrows his eyes at me consideringly.

"You believe that you can help find Methi."

"I sure do. What can it hurt, right?"

A ghost of a smile crosses his face. "I believe it will hurt the egos of my generals if you find Methi before them." His face sobers. "But all that matters is that the ship is located. I will order the Arcav who are currently searching for Methi to allow you access to their files."

I blow out a breath, shoulders slumping in relief.

"Thank you."

Methi

Something splashes my face and I jolt awake, looking up into the eyes of a general I trained myself. I have known Dezi for half a century, and never could I have imagined the look of glee on his face as he stares at me, lying in the dust on a planet that wasn't on our flight plan.

The ship waits just a few hundred lengths away. My jaw clenches at the sight of Talis standing close by. They obviously plan to abandon me here.

I stumble to my feet, head throbbing. "Why?"

Talis snorts. "Is it not obvious? We no longer want Varian's rule. He has grown soft, making treaties with planets that barely offer any advantages. The Arcav could have ruled this galaxy, but he insisted on protecting the weak Fecax and making enemies of the Grivath."

"The Grivath attempted to invade us!"

"Only after their request for a treaty was ignored."

"They run slave planets." I spit. "They have ruined lives

across the universe. They are murderous beasts, and you believe we should have allied with them?"

"Ever the loyal soldier. You sound just like Varian." He throws me a pack. "Water and basic supplies for a few days. You were always good to me. Take this chance."

I just stare at him. "How could you betray us like this? What is your plan? You think Varian will not discover this duplicity?"

Talis grits his teeth. "Varian will not discover anything until it is too late."

I take a step forward, incensed. "You worthless traitor!"

He raises his weapon and pain knifes through my leg as I fall to the ground. I grit my teeth as my nerve endings erupt in fire.

"I am not the worthless one! Perhaps I will take your mouthy human when I arrive back in Arcavia. I will be so devastated that I had to kill the Arcav who was betraying our race. I am sure she will be upset to learn that you were a traitor and tried to kill me. Perhaps she will need...comforting."

I try to ignore his jeering, but my stomach clenches. Would Meghan believe him? I left her with no warning. Would she see that as the act of a traitor?

"No one will believe you," I growl, growing dizzy as my blood saturates the ground beneath me.

"Of course they will. This is the way of the world. I will tell them my sad story and how I discovered your deception. They will be only too happy to believe that the little upstart, the bastard was colluding with the Arcav." He grins down at me. "You should never have dared to crawl so close to the crown," he says, madness dancing across his face. How could I not see this?

"Kill you," I groan weakly, and he simply sneers.

"Goodbye, Methi."

I watch as the ship fires up, Talis and Dezi boarding without looking back. I am sure I will soon lose consciousness, so I pull the bag closer, finding a small bottle of water and some bread.

I use one claw to cut the thick strap off the bag and take a deep breath.

This will hurt.

Talis had landed a glancing blow and his weapon was obviously not fully charged or I would be dead. But I am bleeding heavily enough that my death may be long and painful. I take one breath and bring *her* face to mind. I focus on that quick grin and smart mouth, forcing myself to stay conscious as I sit up.

I will make it back to her.

I take the strap and pull it around the worst of my wound, hoping to replicate the technique Harlow used to slow the bleeding when I was injured just a few short months ago. The gleam of the metal of my arm is a constant reminder of how close I came to death. I wonder if I will lose this leg too. Perhaps I will return to Meghan more metal than male.

Tighten the strap, or you will not return at all.

I cannot afford to scream, in case there are predators nearby. I lean over, biting into the thick material of the bag and groan lowly as I pull the strap tight, tying it in a knot.

I slump down and stare up at the night sky.

I am lying on the ship, a flood of blood escaping my body. I hear Harlow scream, and hope she has the good sense to hide amongst the other humans.

A few moments later, my hopes are quashed, and she crawls

to me as another human provides cover. My King's mate is fierce. I am proud to lay down my life for her.

I groan in pain as she does something that makes my arm burn like fire.

*And then I am awake in the medi-center, meeting **her** for the first time. Her name is Meghan and she is young. So young. But so alive, her innocent eyes staring at me as if we have known each other for our whole lives.*

Harlow says something, but I am no longer listening as Meghan smiles and her face lights up. I harden instantly as those not-so-innocent eyes travel lower to where my sheet is tangled around my waist.

"You left," I mumble aloud. "You left *for her*. Now you will die, and she will never know why. Was it worth it?"

It was.

If I am to die, I am thankful that I got to meet the female who could have been mine. I got to see her for who she is, and I only mourn that I will not get to see who she will one day become.

I keep her face in my mind as the blood loss hits me and I finally lose consciousness.

ALSO BY HOPE HART

The Arcav Alien Invasion Series

The Arcav King's Mate

The Arcav Commander's Human

The Arcav General's Woman

The Arcav Prince's Captive

A Very Arcav Christmas

The Arcav Captain's Queen

The Arcav Guard's Female

The Warriors of Agron Series

Taken by the Alien Warrior

Claimed by the Alien Warrior

Saved by the Alien Warrior

Seduced by the Alien Warrior

Protected by the Alien Warrior

Captured by the Alien Warrior

Rescued by the Alien Warrior

Enticed by the Alien Warrior

Conquered by the Alien Warrior

The Society of Savages Series

Wicked

Depraved

Brutal

Printed in Great Britain
by Amazon